FINAL DECISION

JANET PASSERELL

To my sister Kate, who critiqued, read, re-read, and supported me throughout this process, love and many, many thanks!

To my husband Andy, my children Mike, Andrea, David (and their spouses Wendy, David, and Kim...who I consider "my children") and grandchildren Megan, Lauren, Christina and Chad.....I love you all, "something to remember me by"

PROLOGUE
PRESENT DAY
2003

As she took her seat in first class she thought of all the amazing turns her life had taken. She was now almost 61, a fact she couldn't really accept as she still felt 40. She was about to take another major step in her life, that is if the most important person in her life agreed to meet her upon her arrival in Dulles in approximately 8 hours. Her right hand was grasping a copy of the letter she had sent in preparation for this meeting as she settled into her seat.

She had debated about what to say in this final letter, but ultimately just said what was in her heart and asked for a chance to explain her life, the reasons for the choices she had made, and her undying love for the person she was hopefully about to reconnect with after all these years. She knew the path would not be easy but the next 24 hours would be the "beginning of the rest of her life" as they say, the final phase and ultimately perhaps the most important.

As they reached cruising altitude Carolyn gratefully accepted a glass of wine and plate of cheese and crackers from the steward and sat back to review her life and the unexpected turns it had taken. She knew there would be no sleeping for her on this flight. Her mind wandered back over the events in her life that had brought her to this point, and that fateful decision 21 years ago.

UNIVERSITY OF VIRGINIA
THE EARLY YEARS
1969

Carolyn looked around at the crowded lawn. Roger's residency in General Surgery was over and he was on the brink of joining an established practice in Charlottesville, Virginia. His parents were throwing the final graduation party to welcome their son into the Charlottesville medical community, the party they had long dreamed of giving. The house was on the grounds of the prestigious Charlottesville Country Club and backed up to the 2nd hole of the golf course.

She and Roger had been here for five years now, both having graduated from the University of Pennsylvania, she with her nursing degree and he with his medical degree. It was beginning to feel a bit like home, but still quite a change from her northern upbringing in many ways.

Roger had chosen the University of Virginia for his Residency training mainly because he intended to settle in his home town of Charlottesville and join a General Surgery Practice after graduation. That day was now here. As she watched the people milling around, talking excitedly with each other about their lives she slid off into the library for a bit of quiet reverie and reflection as to the events that had led her to this moment in her life.

She had been brought up as an only child in a very conservative middle class family in New Jersey. Her parents were a happy couple in their own way, had worked hard, never traveled, attended church regularly and led life on the straight and narrow road firmly believing that their reward would come in the after life. This life was but a prelude.

Carolyn was a skinny slightly introverted but intelligent only child, and her parents had great hopes for her future. In those days the hope of most parents was that the next generation would have it a little easier than they did. They being newly middle class envisioned that their only daughter would be the first in the family to get a college education, be exposed to new people, marry well, have children of her own and move up into a world more comfortable and free of the financial worries and stress they had encountered along their way. The goal of the college experience for a woman in her father's view was simply a way of meeting a suitable educated man to marry and raising a happy family as in his mind the purpose of marriage was of course procreation. He was not happy when Carolyn chose nursing as a major, which to him was more of a "service profession," and would rather she had studied music, the arts, or something along those lines to prepare her for the elevated social status he hoped would come with the right marriage. He was also not especially pleased that she had managed a scholarship to a secular college preferring she stay within the confines of a church related school, however it was a good school and the money certainly helped so he had soon relented and off she went to the University of Pennsylvania.

Her education to this point had been under the scrutiny of the Catholic Church right through high school. Her experience with religion from the nuns and priests in the '50's was based entirely on fear of eternal damnation for anyone who strayed off the straight and narrow path of righteousness and dared to break the church's rules. She learned not of a loving God but of a God who only let the perfect people and the repentant sinners into heaven for a joyful afterlife. The rest, including those who were unfortunate enough to die before having the chance to repent for their transgressions, were sent to eternal damnation. She came out of this religious upbringing with a great fear of doing something wrong, a strong sense of guilt when she had done wrong, and of wanting to be perfect not only so her parents would be proud of her but also so she would be rewarded in another life after she died. This type of thinking all ended when upon entering her second year of college she met a senior business major named Andrew Romano.

He was unlike anyone she had ever known in her life thus far. He was from a close Italian family. He was everything she wasn't: street smart, fun loving, with apparently not a care in the world. His life was joyous; he had no fears, no conscience dictating how his life was to be lived. His only goal was to live life to the fullest 24 hours a day. His family had a history of early deaths from heart disease and Andrew had decided he was going to have as much fun and see as much of the world as he could while he was young and healthy if an early demise was to be his fate. He did not believe in an afterlife.

They had dated for a year and he had totally changed Carolyn's life. He introduced her to a world she hadn't even imagined could exist, a carefree world full of fun and excitement. He helped her to balance the seriousness and responsibilities of the issues she dealt with daily in her hospital training program with the life she should be experiencing as a newly independent young woman.

They talked for hours throughout the nights about life subjects, ideas and philosophies that had only been skimmed over in her superficial relationships with other people. They partied hard, he introduced her to hiking, camping, political rallies (he was far more liberal than she of course and they had spirited debates in this area), fraternity parties, rock concerts and her first sexual experience. She remembered how she had fretted for months over the decision to "sleep with him" as was the euphemism in those days for sexual relations. She was probably the only virgin on campus; this was the "60's" after all. Carolyn smiled to herself as she remembered the three day religious retreat she went on while struggling with that momentous decision.

She had been totally and completely in love with him that year and happier than she had ever thought possible. They promised to love each other always, and as soon as she graduated would explore the world together stopping wherever and whenever the urge hit them. It had been the happiest year of her life thus far. She remembered how distraught and fearful her parents were regarding this relationship. Her good Irish-American parents insisted that Andrew and she were from two different worlds and that they would ultimately with time find they had nothing in common. After all, not only was he a non- practicing Catholic, but also Italian!

After Andrew graduated he took a job in Sales and Marketing for an Advertising firm in New York City at which he was perfect. They had decided that whatever he could make while waiting for Carolyn to finish up her two remaining years of school they would use as their nest egg for their world adventures. The plan had gone well for the first few months. Being in the nursing program she did not get a summer break, this time was used for "clinical experience," in other words the students provided free staffing to the hospital while the hospital provided real life clinical experience. Andrew returned to visit every weekend at first, then monthly, then every other month. Then came a chance for him to work for an International Advertising firm in London and he left excitedly promising that the money would be great and after she graduated she could join him and start their adventures. They kept in touch with phone calls and letters, but the intervals between contact became longer and longer. By the beginning of her senior year Andrew had disappeared from her life. Carolyn was devastated and depressed. She decided Andrew had been her "temptation" and she had failed. It was time to get back on the straight and narrow road to her real life's vocation. She devoted herself entirely to her studies.

Enter Roger, tall dashing good looking med student in his final year of internship. It was her last year of nursing school. Roger was proper, very conservative, from a wealthy southern family, had a good future ahead and treated her with respect and like a queen. Her parents adored him and saw a financially secure life ahead for their daughter and hopefully their future grandchildren. The M.D. behind his name guaranteed to them that he would provide the life they envisioned for their daughter's future. This even trumped the fact that he was a Southern WASP and not a Catholic. Carolyn became more and more "fond" of Roger and comfortable with him. She decided this was probably a more sensible path to follow. Can you say Rebound?????

They had been in Virginia five years while he completed his General Surgery Residency, though not the Deep South nonetheless it was the south. Roger had agreed to her working while he was in his Residency but only in an "acceptable" position, he didn't want his wife doing basic bedside nursing in a hospital. She therefore got a position as an office nurse for a young Family Practice physician who had also done his residency at the University of Virginia where he had met his wife. Carolyn loved her job, got totally involved with her patients and their families. She and Jeff Mullins became quite good friends and a great team in treating their patients with knowledge, care and respect. Jeff's wife Terri was his office manager, a nurse herself, and soon became Carolyn's closest confidant. Jeff had graduated three years ahead of Roger from their undergraduate studies at the University of Virginia before they went off to separate med schools. They had been in the TKE fraternity together so it was easy for Roger and Jeff to renew their social ties and a perfect opportunity for Carolyn to develop a close friendship with Terri. They were a happy five years.

As she had glanced through the library window at "Charlottesville's upper crust medical community" on the lawn celebrating Roger's pending entrance into their ranks she knew her life was once again slated to change. Roger had made it clear that once he was out in "the real world" practicing surgery that she should give up her office job and spend her time setting up a home for them and nurturing suitable social contacts. Thus to that end his parents' graduation gift to Roger was membership in the local country club where they would begin their upscale climb and associate with the right people now that Roger's schedule would be more amenable to socializing. After all, he was entering a Surgery Practice affiliated with the local community hospital as a junior partner and in that field would have fairly regular daytime hours for the most part. Most of the trauma victims requiring emergency surgery would likely be taken to the larger University Hospital. She was very proud of Roger, from what she had seen and had heard from several sources he was a very caring and skilled surgeon, but she wasn't too sure she was thrilled about her end of the bargain. However, she did want a family and how could she complain about financially not having to work and having the leisure time to establish a secure and happy life for them and their future family. She knew however she would miss working with Terri and Jeff, and most especially miss the contact with the patients. Terri on the other hand was quickly encouraging her to become part of the women's golf group at the club so they could start playing golf together on a more regular basis. They were presently living in the guest cottage on Roger's parents' property and since this was located within the gated country club community they had already established some social contacts and she had learned to play golf and tennis as a guest courtesy of her father-in- law's membership.

She emerged from the library back to the lawn to partake fully in the celebration, this was Roger's day and he deserved her support. She vowed to herself to start house hunting the following week. It was finally time to really spring out on their own, how could she not look forward to that! She was to no longer be the nurse she had studied to be and though she would miss that part of her life greatly, she was now to be the family social manager, cultivate new friendships both business and social, and build a life of their own. The subject of a family was a different matter. They had discussed starting a family once Roger was more established perhaps, though a small one. She had always envisioned three to five children, Roger was more inclined toward possibly one as he wanted to "live the good life," travel and see the world in their free time. She would work on that later, first decision was where to live. He wanted a house within the gated country club area, close to the hospital, she wanted a house in the country perhaps on the James River nearby where they could have some privacy away from the "club friendships" and have room for kids and dogs. She wanted their future children to be exposed to a more diverse group of people than they would find within the confines of the Country Club gates. The battle lines had been established.

COUNTRY CLUB LIFE
TEN YEARS LATER......1979

"Just consider it!" begged Jenny. They were sitting on the patio outside the 19th hole after having just beaten their fiercest rival club team for the Ladies Golf League championship. It was a gorgeous day with clear blue sky, no humidity and Carolyn had just shot the best score of her short golf career. She was content and seemingly happy but still felt something was missing in her life. If someone had told her ten years ago after joining the Country Club and starting to play golf that her game would have progressed this far she would never have believed it. She also wouldn't have believed she was so passionate about the game. She who had never been athletic was now one of the top players on the B league team, with a respectable handicap of 20. If she could lower it just a bit more she would be able to join the A team next season. It was a goal she had been pursuing with zest.

She enjoyed playing golf with Jenny, yet they were as different as two people could possibly be. Jenny was by all standards a very attractive 42-year-old woman who had been brought up in a country club environment being the daughter of a local lawyer who happened to be Roger's father's law partner. Jenny and Roger had gone to high school together and then dated while they were both undergrads at U.Va., traveled in the same social circles, but lost touch when he moved on to Medical School at the University of Pennsylvania. She stayed local after graduating with an accounting degree, became a CPA and with the help of her dad's business and club contacts as clients, now owned a very successful accounting firm specializing in taxes, estate planning etc.. She had been married briefly which didn't work out, got a nice settlement from her very wealthy ex-husband and now lived very comfortably with golf and travel as her main passions and the country club life as her existence. She still owned the firm but had no hands-on duties. She dated when the opportunity arose and the prospect met her criteria: wealthy, attractive and interesting. However she fully planned to remain a single woman. She loved her independence. She had taken Carolyn under her wing ten years ago when she and Roger joined the club as sort of a favor to an old friend, and actually as Carolyn had soon discovered Jenny and Roger had been much more than friends but that was many many years ago. Surprisingly to them both Jenny and Carolyn had discovered they had much in common. Golf of course became the avenue for the friendship starting, but they were both avid readers, loved nature and the outdoors, gardening, animals etc.

What Jenny was trying to talk Carolyn into considering was that a few of the C'ville CC women's golf team, both A and B players, were planning a golf trip to Scotland and Jenny thought it the perfect opportunity for her to travel, see a little of the outside world and get to know some of the A players better so she would hopefully be able to join them next season as part of the team. Jenny was already definitely moving up to the A team.

"Just think about it," Jenny insisted. "Even Terri is going to join us on this one and if she can leave Jeff for a few weeks you can certainly abandon your hubby for that short time." She smiled as she said it, but Carolyn knew that Jenny would think it quite pathetic if she knew that she only ever traveled when Roger accompanied her.

Carolyn was not so sure about the trip. Truth was she wasn't all that keen on flying though she tried to keep that to herself as amongst their friends that would be looked on as sort of bizarre. She was actually very content with her life as it was for now. She still very much wanted to start a family, however Roger always seemed to be putting that decision off a little into the future while not ruling it out entirely. They were fortunate to not have to struggle financially and she would be able to be a "stay at home" mom, a thought she treasured. The social life although fun was becoming a bit empty. She was 37 now and didn't want to wait too much longer before starting their family. She talked with Jenny about all these feelings.

"All the more reason for participating in this trip" was Jenny's reply, "knowing you, once you start raising those precious future kiddies you will probably never leave them until they are out of college." She said this good heartedly but also with a bit of disdain for someone who wanted only to be a mom and raise kids. Her true intent was to convince Carolyn that there was so much more to life than raising kids. Carolyn had become one of her most loyal friends. Raising a family was also just not one of Jenny's goals in life so she also had a hard time empathizing with Carolyn on this subject. Jenny hung out with a wealthy fast moving traveling active crowd and had no desire for a husband or children to slow her down. Although she truly loved her life she was so self-centered, outspoken, and convinced she was always right all the time that she had a hard time holding onto long term friendships and therefore she treasured her relatively long-term relationship with Carolyn all the more. There was of course another more important reason she wanted Carolyn to forget about "the family idea." Jenny knew for a fact that Roger was never going to have children.

"All right, I will consider it". Carolyn stated meekly, I will talk with Roger when the moment is right.

"Great, I just happen to have a copy of the entire travel package details in the car for you to take home and browse through". You know Roger is so involved with his Practice, his tennis and squash and golf life, he won't miss you if you disappear for two weeks or so. You owe it to yourself while you are still not tied down with family obligations, and perhaps he will miss you so much he will be ready to start a family when you return so as to assure you will never leave him again". Again said in jest, but to Carolyn it planted a seed.

They finished lunch, Carolyn took the travel info package and headed home promising to call Jenny in the next couple of days with a decision. She contemplated where she was in her life on the drive home. She was not unhappy with Roger, but they were leading a somewhat superficial life. They were entrenched in a busy social life at the club. Roger was busy with his Practice, they had hired a younger partner so there were now more of them to share the "on-call" nights and that had greatly increased Roger's free time. He was now more than ever enjoying his sports and friendships at the club. She was busy building them a life outside his work and admittedly enjoying her golf life as well. Most of their conversations related to their social schedules. Their sex life was good, but even at 42, with his busy schedule Roger was seeming a little less interested these days. To be honest he seemed to look forward to his tennis, squash, golf and card games at the club with the guys more than to their more and more infrequent quiet romantic evenings at home. She on the other hand treasured their alone time at home. Although they participated in the occasional mixed foursome golf events they didn't really spend a lot of time together even at the club except for dinners and special events with their mutual friends.

Their first real public disagreement had been in regards to the racial issue brewing at the club at present. The University in Charlottesville had recently let it be known that they would prefer their professors and staff should not be seen as members of an all white country club, just not a good image for a public university. While most of the country had moved past all white clubs more than a decade ago, not as true in some parts of the south, including Virginia. A good portion of Roger's colleagues at the hospital had resigned from the club in compliance with the University position, Roger on the other hand thought the whole issue was ridiculous. As he stated there was nothing in the club bylaws that stated a person of any particular race or color could not be a member of the club. What the bylaws simply stated was that a person wishing to join the club must be sponsored by an existing member, seconded by another member and presented to the board for approval. It was then the board's decision whether to accept the person as a member or not. One negative vote was enough to disqualify a person and the reason for rejection would not be made public even to the applicants themselves. As the members owned the club it was therefore private they could legally set their own rules. This was becoming a source of great debate regarding diversity and more open policies as people from all over joined their growing University based town, parents of U. Va. Students joined as out-of-town members, and younger couples joined the club as the economy was good and middle class people could afford to belong to a country club now. Carolyn and Roger were definitely on opposite sides and he was not pleased that she was making her feelings known. As she pointed out even if no stated policy existed, there were no people of color, no people of the Jewish faith, in fact she was probably the only Catholic member although these days she was not practicing her faith outwardly. When she began to look at the membership more closely it seemed not even a person of any different nationality, i.e. Italian, Indian, Asian or Irish had broken the barrier as yet. The club was an old money club with mainly a WASP membership. This was becoming an area where their inherent differences were starting to come to the surface.

On the positive side Roger had given in to her and let her choose their place of residence. They had purchased a small house about 40 minutes outside of town on about 25 acres bordering on the James River. It was her dream property, quiet, private, lots of room for gardening and playing with their two golden retrievers. They had cleared walking paths from the house down to the dock and she loved her long walks with the dogs, watching the seasons change, and had even become an avid bird watcher. Life was going well but not exactly as she had imagined. They kept a small condo in town where Roger could stay if he worked especially late and when the weather was bad as the road to the river was small and curvy, or if they had a particularly long social event and just didn't feel like driving the country roads after drinking perhaps a bit too much wine they both crashed at the condo, although their social life was becoming more and more sedate lately. She was also pursuing her "secret life" of writing short stories and articles mostly for women's magazines and nature magazines under the alias Sara Church. Writing was her second career choice and she had shared this with no one. At that time she had no idea what a major role this would play in her future. For now it was just an enjoyable private pastime.

Roger had a hospital meeting that evening and she made herself a salad and along with some fresh bread, cheese, a bottle of Chardonnay and the newspaper and headed down to the dock to read, relax and watch the sun begin to descend into the river. She found it hard to concentrate on the newspaper though and instead began to imagine taking that trip to Scotland with Jenny and her golf league partners. She scurried back up to the car and brought the travel packet back down to the dock with her. The trip included going to four different courses in a period of 21 days in order to see the different terrains of Scotland. They would start at Turnberry on the south western side, on to Glenn Eagles in central Scotland, to St. Andrews of course on the eastern side, and then up to the highlands for a taste of the more rural northern part of the country. They would fly in and out of Heathrow and thus have a couple of days in London before returning home. Perhaps she should consider it, she had grown to love the golf and never having been competitive in anything before she was finding herself actually caring whether she won or not and even enjoying the struggle to lower that precious handicap. It might even put a spark back into their marriage, as Jenny had implied, if they had the chance to be apart for a short while. She wasn't sure how Roger would react to the idea. She let her mind wander as she finished her salad, listened to the water ripple over the rocks in the river and watched the sun disappear. Rusty and Randy laid on the river bank after frolicking in the water and she watched as they shook themselves dry. For retrievers they paid little attention to the occasional bird or rabbit that passed by and even less to the jumping fish.

THE GOLF TRIP
SCOTLAND

Six weeks later she found herself pulling into Dulles airport with Jenny for the flight to London and then after a short layover on to Glasgow where their golf adventure would begin. Roger had been just fine with the trip. He had liked the idea of her getting closer with the women of some of the more influential families in Albemarle County, it was good for his Practice and his referrals. He preferred her keeping company with these people rather than the "rural" people by the river with whom she actually was more comfortable. She was seeing more and more a side of him she was not exactly fond of. The women had all individually made their travel arrangements and the eight of them were independently flying to Glasgow via Heathrow and meeting at Turnberry. She and Jenny were traveling together.

Did she dare tell anyone this was her first oversees flight? Her companions were all well-seasoned travelers having mostly grown up in the country club atmosphere and gone to colleges where they had done semesters in other countries. She had done some traveling with Roger to conferences in different states and flown to some of the Caribbean islands for vacations but no international flying and actually no flying at all without Roger. She was feeling quite the country bumpkin and decided to keep her mouth shut and hide her trepidations about sitting for six hours at 35,000 feet over that huge blue expanse of water in a metal tube filled with gallons of fuel.

She actually would have preferred to have Terri as her traveling partner but had let Jenny take care of all the travel arrangements as she enjoyed doing that sort of thing. Jenny had also researched the hotels, the golf courses etc., etc., etc. Carolyn's mother would have been proud of her going off on her own, her father would have shuddered to think that she was leaving her husband alone even if only for three weeks to do something so frivolous. They had both passed away over the previous ten years, but had died proud of the life they saw her embracing. They had been very impressed with Roger since the beginning, although they had not lived long enough to see a first grandchild be born that they had so longed for, and this she would always regret. Roger's parents had retired to a golfing community in Florida and then also had passed away a few years ago. There would be no grandparents in the picture for their future children. She was not going to dwell on that right now.

"I have a surprise for you" Jenny was saying as they were approaching the ticket counter. "I have gotten us an upgrade to first class, figured it would be worth it to get a good night's rest."

Yes, Carolyn was ready for her first overseas adventure as an independent woman and she intended to make the most of this trip and put all other thoughts and future plans on hold for the next three weeks. "Live in the present" as her yoga instructor would insist.

She and Jenny checked in and settled into their very comfortable seats, now this was what flying was supposed to be like, large comfortable reclining seats, lots of leg room, the steward offered them some wine or champagne as they reached their cruising altitude, and later after dinner and a movie, brought them footies and a small cosmetic bag with toiletries to refresh themselves before sleeping. Perhaps she could get used to this life she thought. The flight went smoothly and quickly and before she realized it they were landing. At Heathrow they transferred to a smaller plane and when they landed shortly thereafter in Glasgow Carolyn was relaxed and eager for her first real solo adventure. She was already beginning to feel like the "jet set" life may be fun after all.

Glasgow was a very industrial city and they quickly rented a car and headed south to Turnberry where they were meeting up with the other six women in their group. Jenny once again took charge offering to drive, since it was "left side of the road" driving. Carolyn had no problem deferring to her. It was only a few hours before they pulled into the ancient Turnberry Lodging. The view was magnificent. It was so clear they could actually see Ireland in the distance. Now this was the Scotland of her imagination, green grass, stately old hotel with enormous columns and brick porches and a grand entrance with white columns and brick steps. The sky a perfect shade of blue. They settled quickly into their rooms having learned some of their other friends had arrived the day before and while Carolyn took a shower and unpacked Jenny went down to the pro shop to make sure all the arrangements were in place for golf the next day. She had made tee times at all four locations and they would alternate who played in which foursome. It was going to be a busy few weeks and Carolyn was looking forward to immersing herself in golf, the countryside, the history of Scotland, and thinking of nothing else. All other decisions could wait until her return. She joined the rest of the group in the library for cocktails after which they dined in the stately dining room filled with old mahogany furniture, fine china and fair food as the Scots were not exactly known for their cuisine. As the darkness fell they watched the ceremonial bagpipe player traverse the porch outside serenading in the evening sunset.   What an absolutely perfect beginning.

The next morning as she approached the first tee Carolyn quickly realized she was a bit out of her level of golf expertise, but even this did not dampen her enthusiasm. She knew the course would be hilly and the rough thick.   What she wasn't prepared for was the extent of the cold force of the wind. She could barely get her drive over the mounds of heather grass, and when they saw that the wind was so strong it was actually moving the ball on the putting surface the women all decided they would be putting in no scores on this trip. It was a time to just enjoy the moment. They had had to have the golf pro at the club certify their handicaps so that they were low enough to even play on some of the Scottish courses such as St. Andrews, and they were sure the caddies did not believe the numbers submitted as most surely none of them were playing to their handicaps that day. In fact when prior to a shot Carolyn asked her caddie if he thought a 7 iron was the correct club, the caddie replied politely, "How far do you hit your 7 iron?"

"Actually I have no idea," was her reply, "I just go by how far it looks to me to the target."

With that the caddie rolled his eyes and she heard him mumble under his breath "This is going to be a very long day!" If he only knew she had never even played a round of golf with a caddie before, she was sure he would be even more exasperated. She thankfully hit a beautiful and very lucky 7 iron shot.

Carolyn was as content that afternoon as she had been in ages and living in the moment for the first time in a long time with no planning going on in her head, just enjoying the present. She admitted to the group that this was the first time she had been separated from her husband due to her own travel plans. Roger of course had been to medical meetings and golf trips without her. In her late 30's she was beginning to feel like a liberated teenager if only for two weeks. The next day would be free for sightseeing or just relaxing. She was enjoying the company of the other women, but also secretly hoping to get to play in Terri's foursome at Glenn Eagles, which was to be their next course.

Two days later as they entered the grounds of Glenn Eagles, the second course on their agenda, Carolyn felt that this would not be her favorite stop. It was a magnificent stone lodging with manicured lawns, fountains, and marble lobby but the kind of atmosphere and luxurious surroundings that could have been found anywhere in the world including Virginia. She had come to Scotland to see something different. She was already enthralled and captivated by the countryside, the rolling hills, the narrow roads bordered by old stone walls, the clear streams. They had arranged to "sight see" on their own between courses and had broken into pairs, she with Jenny, each two women having their own rental car and they would just meet at the next course on the schedule for dinner the night before they played. She was already finding herself much more excited about the exploring than the golf. She was avidly reading everything she could get her hands on about the areas they would be seeing. Selfishly she kind of wished she was "paired" with Terri to sightsee as well, as they were closer friends than she and Jenny, but c'est la vie! Jenny had certainly been pleasant enough, and flexible in their arrangements.

After checking into their room Carolyn told Jenny she was going to the practice range to stretch and hit a few balls before dinner and she would meet the group at 7 in the dining room.

She was completely into her practice routine, starting as always with the shortest iron and working her way up to the driver which she was presently hitting when she was startled by an old but immediately familiar voice behind her saying "Could this possibly be the totally non athletic woman I once knew many years ago?" She turned to face Andrew Romano.

Her heart was beating much too fast and she felt herself spiralling a bit out of control. It was ridiculous that he should have this much of an impact on her after all these years. Knowing him as thoroughly as she once had, as she turned with a sweet fake smile and a trembling voice all she could get out was "This is much too weird to be a coincidence!"

"Well, not altogether a surprise on my part I must admit. May I buy you a glass of wine and allow me to satisfy your curiosity which I have obviously succeeded in arousing?"

He looked amazing, the only change being the specks of white beginning to show in his hair. She immediately felt self-conscious about the approximately 10 pounds she had taken on in the last ten years with all the good food and wine she had been consuming. She allowed him to help her gather her clubs together and managed to get to the table on the patio without letting him see how her entire body was trembling inside, heart racing and legs weak. How dare he still have this effect on her after all these years!

Two bottles of fine white wine later, which she had allowed him to choose, and some wonderful appetizers they spent the next two hours catching up with each other's lives, although it would take much more time than that to explain all the emotions that had occurred on both sides. Short explanation: he was now marketing director for a large international advertising agency and one of his largest accounts was the cruise industry. He traveled constantly but maintained apartments in both London and in Olde Town, Alexandria right outside Washington D.C. He vacationed frequently at Glenn Eagles where a friend of his, Ian McDonald, was the director of golf. Ian had gotten Andrew interested in golf many years ago and now the sport was a passion of Andrew's as well. Andrew had seen the tee times marked off for the "Charlottesville, Virginia" group in his friend's office weeks ago and knowing that that was where she had settled he had searched the listing hoping beyond hope that her name would be on the reservation list. He had kept in touch with enough UP alumni news to know that that was where she and Roger had settled and he knew that he just had to see her. He had followed her life in the states when he could, at least knew that she had married Roger and was living in Virginia. He found himself desperately wanting to know more. He couldn't explain it after all these years but his spirits soared when he found she would be there at least for one night. He explained that he had been in several relationships over the past decade or so but with all the travel and business obligations that he had never really settled down, and actually was enjoying being free to see the world. She couldn't help but think that that had been their plan, hadn't it, to see the world together when she had graduated! A taste of bitterness swelled within her.

"I have an idea" she heard Andrew saying as she tried to keep this meeting light. "My understanding is that your foursome's are teeing off at 9 and 9:15 tomorrow morning, is there any chance that I could take you to a late lunch after that? I would love to show you the countryside and talk some more. She too would love that she thought, but how do I casually say yes her mind was saying as her voice spoke out clearly "That would be lovely, I would enjoy that." She found herself explaining their itinerary and how they played the course

29

one day and then had a day or sometimes two on their own to sightsee before meeting up at the next course. She could only blame the wine for her quick acceptance.

At dinner that night she explained to Jenny and the rest of the group that as unbelievable as it sounded she had met an old college friend who was also staying at Glenn Eagles and they were going to spend the afternoon sightseeing after golf the next day. Jenny took it very much in stride and stated she had already decided she was going to spend the afternoon at the Spa relaxing and getting a massage rather than doing any more sightseeing. Ironically no one even asked the gender of the former friend and Carolyn was happy and relieved not to have to provide any further information.

The weather was much improved the next morning as the group met on the first tee. Glenn Eagles was not a seaside course and thus not as windy as Turnberry had been. Once again Jenny had taken the initiative to pair them with different partners than they had played with in their previous round just to mix things up a bit. This time Terri was in her foursome. This course was much more manageable than Turnberry, which lifted all of their golf confidence levels.

"Any chance that old friend could be the handsome gentleman I saw you with on the patio yesterday afternoon?" Terri said with a slightly interested smirk.

Carolyn laughed and said yes, that he was a long ago friend from college and smiled saying "you know that was like a different lifetime, but he lives in London now and is quite familiar with the region around

Gleneagles and so is the perfect guide since I have such a short time to see the area." Carolyn was no longer nervous about her upcoming meeting with Andrew, to the contrary she was actually relaxed, played well, and she was looking forward to seeing the sights with somewhat of a "local" as a guide. After all, her romance with Andrew was well in the past and there was no reason two old friends couldn't have a pleasant day together. She had to admit she was also curious about what was happening in his present life.

After golf she informed the rest of the group that she would not be joining them for dinner, since she was reasonably sure she would be having dinner with Andrew. She told Jenny she would see her later that evening.

Andrew was looking rather dashing in his casual sports shirt and khaki's as he picked her up in his small BMW convertible. "I thought we would have a picnic and take advantage of the gorgeous clear afternoon, they are not always so lucky with the weather around here. I took the liberty of having the hotel pack us some food and wine if that is alright with you?"

"Lovely" was all she could manage to get out well aware that she was overusing that particular word, while her thoughts went back to how much they used to enjoy eating outside back in their college courtship days. Roger hated even eating out on the back deck because it was always too hot, too buggy, too windy or whatever other excuse he could come up with. He much preferred the sterile atmosphere of the indoor air-conditioning. In fact on busy days he had taken more and more to staying at their in-town condo near the hospital rather than driving to the river property. Carolyn put her head back against the seat and let her hair fly loosely as they drove into the countryside for their picnic by a stream. After lunch Andrew true to his work took her to some nearby sights: Loch Lomond, Scone Palace, Stirling Castle, Pitlochry. She was feeling 10 years younger already.

The conversation flowed easily, they talked about the golf holes on the King's course, Carolyn joked that she wished she had had him as a caddie or at least that she had gotten all this inside info on where to hit etc. and how to play each hole. She told him how upset her caddie had been at Turnberry at finding himself spending the morning caddying for a woman whose golf game was mediocre at best. How funny that each of them was so passionate about a sport they had actually paid little if no attention to until well into their adult lives. Of course there were some awkward moments also when they would start reminiscing about the "good old days" at college and then remember how badly it had ended for them. Andrew made no big apologies about his eventual disappearance from her life although he had to know how hurt she had been. It was just the way it turned out back many years ago, that was then and this was now. Somehow she was not able to dismiss the way their lives separated so easily but restrained herself from saying so and vowed to continue "living in the moment." She had barely even thought about Roger since the trip began. She did miss the retrievers and her quiet spot on the river.

As they returned to the hotel that evening Andrew surprised her by asking her if it would be possible to spend more time together before her return to the states. She explained the group would be heading on to St. Andrews in the morning, had a free day there followed by golf on the Old Course the next day. After that up to Dornoch for a taste of golf in the highlands and then on to some free time, meeting up with the group in Edinburgh before heading to London for two days of sightseeing. She could see the unmistakable pleasure in his face when she told him her return flight home was actually from Heathrow and so she would have a couple of free days in London.

"Perfect!" he said not even trying to hide his enthusiasm. "If you agree, I will meet you in Edinburgh and we could take the train down to London, a nice way to see the countryside scenery, and I would love it if you would stay with me in London and allow me to show you a bit of the city sights."

"Whoa, aren't we forgetting I am a married woman whom you have not even spoken to or seen in many years. I have no idea of your living arrangements, your life over the past ten plus years, and really don't think I want to be jumping into staying with you after a brief one day rendezvous."

"Now that sounds like the naïve sheltered young lady I first met many years ago before you blossomed into the wonderful intelligent worldly woman I fell in love with many moons ago." He said this with quite a grin, the grin that had first attracted her to him.

"Let me explain," he continued a bit more seriously, "I certainly didn't mean to jump ahead like that or sound like I was assuming that you were on a girls trip because you were a wealthy bored housewife looking for an exciting vacation affair. I am merely offering an opportunity for two old friends to catch up with each other's lives, and since I have an apartment in London and know the city well and happen to be a wonderful travel guide, I think I can help you make the most of your first trip here". He went on to explain that although it was a one bedroom apartment it did include an office with a sofa bed where he would properly sleep for the two nights he hoped she would stay with him and allow him to show her the sights.

Carolyn had to admit there was nothing she would rather do than find out what he had been up to these past years and actually see where he was living. After all, what harm in seeing London with a semi-local resident. She did realize in that moment that there was no way Roger would not know of this side trip, as Jenny, not to mention the other women were not ones to keep secrets. She had to think about this.

"I will give you the number of the hotel in Edinburgh, let me think about this for a couple of days. It has been nice seeing you again and I will contact you with our arrival date and see what we can arrange." She gave him a smile and friendly kiss on the cheek and headed into the hotel lobby alone. Only then did she see her women's group emerging from the hotel for a walk onto the grounds.

REUNITING WITH ANDREW ONE WEEK LATER

She and Jenny were just checking into their room in Edinburgh when she saw the blinking red message light on the phone. Her first thought was of Roger, but when she picked up the hotel phone it was Andrew's voice greeting her on the recording. "I will pick you up for dinner tonight at 8pm if that suits, we have train reservations for Tuesday afternoon to London which will give me time to show you a quick overview of Edinburgh and still have daylight to see the scenery between here and London." If you agree please call room 406 when you get this message."

"How arrogant!" she blurted out.

"Must be the mystery man" Jenny replied with a knowing grin. You obviously haven't stopped thinking about him since we left Glenn Eagles, so I can't imagine that you aren't thrilled that he called."

She had not been able to keep the visit with Andrew to herself for long. Jenny and the other ladies were returning from dinner at Glenn Eagles when Andrew had dropped her off in his shiny little BMW after their day of picnicking and sightseeing. Both she and Andrew were feeling very sociable having had quite a bit of wine throughout the day and Andrew easily charmed them all. The secret was out, Carolyn's "friend" was an old college beau. Over the course of the next few days she had told Jenny and Terri the entire story of her college romance.

"He doesn't have to take it for granted that I am just waiting for him to call! This is too weird and surreal and going at way too fast a pace."

"Weren't you hoping for this call and the chance to spend more time with him?" replied Jenny with a smile. "He's not asking you to sleep with him, just two former friends getting together one last time, right?" You could see the mischief in her eyes as she was thoroughly enjoying Carolyn's discomfort. "If you don't want to meet him I certainly am willing to take your place and take my chances. He is gorgeous, and after all I am a free woman." She smiled teasingly, watching and observing Carolyn's embarrassment and ambivalence.

Carolyn settled down as she unpacked. After all if she was honest with herself this was exactly what she was hoping would happen. She had basically thought about Andrew the entire past week and her golf scores certainly showed that she wasn't concentrating on her game, although she was enthralled with the places she had seen, especially Dornoch, the small town in the Highlands. She recalled how sleeping under her down quilt with the window open in her room listening to the waves and enjoying the breezes from the North Sea she had thought of Andrew and how amazing that this trip had offered the unbelievable chance of a reunion with him. Of course she wanted to see him again, but what then?

After settling down a bit and with Jenny's encouragement, "Why deny yourself the chance of getting the answers to what has happened to Andrew since those college years?" Carolyn picked up the phone and asked for room 406.

THE NEXT FEW DAYS

They strolled through the city that evening and he took her to a local pub for dinner. It was so easy falling back into opening up and voicing her true feelings to him. She and Roger hadn't really "talked" for a long time with him being caught up in his Practice and she pursuing golf, settling the house, running their social life etc etc etc. They had even cultivated different friendships although they tried to combine them in their social invitations.

After dinner Andrew surprised her once again. "Have you ever heard of the Military Tattoo that takes place in Edinburgh once a year?"

She looked at him expectantly, not sure if this was a joke, a test of her worldly knowledge so he could make fun of her naiveté, or a serious question. "No" was all she could get out.

"Well it is a once a year festival held outdoors at Edinburgh Palace and quite a sight to behold. They invite military bands from all over Europe to perform in the outdoor arena on the grounds of Edinburgh Castle. Most tickets are sold a year in advance."

"…and?" She questioned. She knew of course the answer to this question, Andrew had always managed to get last minute tickets to any sold out event, as his gift of gab had endeared him to lots of people and he had always had "connections," so why should she suppose that that had not changed.

When she looked back at him he was holding two tickets.

"The only problem is that the castle is several blocks away and there will be huge crowds." He signaled for the check and they took off like two teenagers to get to the performance. She couldn't remember when she last did something spontaneous, she and Roger planned their social events weeks if not months ahead and everything was organized to perfection. She had to admit she was thoroughly enjoying herself leaving all the arrangements up to Andrew. They had wonderful seats and the music and pageantry was amazing. It sent chills through her when the performance ended under a star-lit sky with a single bagpiper in the castle tower playing Amazing Grace on his bugle. The night was magical and she left with tears streaming down her eyes huddled happily against Andrew's warm embrace.

There was no way to keep it secret about where she was headed this time. She just had to trust that Jenny and her other companions would not blurt things out to Roger on their return before she had a chance to talk with him. Although she had grown fond of Jenny in many ways over the years, she did keep in mind that club gossip was a great past time of hers. She knew the only person to whom she could truly confide her feelings would be Terri and she just could not find the right moment to catch her alone so she could bounce her thoughts off of her. She fully intended to tell Roger about meeting Andrew and how things had turned out. Andrew and Roger had never met since Andrew was out of the picture by the time Roger entered her life, but after all this was just an innocent meeting of two old college friends wasn't it? She decided she was going to enjoy this respite from her ordinary "real life" and simply told the ladies she would meet them at Heathrow for the flight home in a few days. Andrew always did make her feel adventurous.

They toured Edinburgh on foot the next morning with Andrew being the perfect guide showing her the sights and filling her in on the local lore. After which they headed to the train station. On the trip to London she told him of her golf games and sightseeing over the past week. He let her go on and on about the beauty of the town of St. Andrews and her amazement of how the course ran through the very center of the village even including a walking path from the center of the village to the sea across the last few holes. He encouraged her rambling and was the perfect listener. The conversation flowed easily with her doing most of the talking and Andrew filling in some non-touristy informative tidbits about places she had seen over the last few days, making her wish he had been with her and making her look forward to his being her personal tour guide in London. He made her feel interesting, listening to every word she said.

As Carolyn went on and on regarding the golf, the sightseeing, her emotions at seeing different terrains, the train trip passed quickly without her really seeing much of the countryside. They had a lovely lunch in the dining car along with a decent bottle of wine. Carolyn was fully engrossed in her present situation and determined not to read anything into it, just following the

Buddhist tradition of forgetting the past, not worrying about the future, and just living in the present. This had become her new mantra, at least for the next week.

Andrew's apartment was small but attractive and as he had promised he moved his things into his office space with the sofa bed while she set up in the main bedroom. He took her on a whirlwind tour of the London sights over the next two days including the Tower of London, Buckingham Palace, Hyde park where they watched people standing on boxes proclaiming their political views or just ranting on about anything that was on their mind...after which she and Andrew got into a political discussion of current worldwide events and British politics versus American...She felt like they were back in college discussing the issues of the day, and that her opinion actually mattered to him. She of course had to do some shopping at Harrods, where she was totally blown away when she saw that there was an entire floor in the famous department store devoted to meats and other foods! She was also quite bemused by the people selling "knock-off" jewelry illegally on the street corners and how they quickly folded up their wares and disappeared into the crowd when a Bobbie showed up close by. These hustlers were a step upscale and a lot more organized than the peddlers of the New York City she had seen. He even took her to the theater as he said you couldn't fully see London without seeing the theater, and then back to the hotel via the underground tube which at just before midnight was quite clean and safe, something she would never have done on trips to NYC with Roger as he would have considered it not only dangerous but quite below their state in life, no she and Roger would have been properly transported back to their hotel in a cab, if not a private limo. The conversation flowed freely, they talked a bit about the past and how he had disappeared (he was just too young to settle down and felt he wasn't right for her but had missed her terribly over the ensuing years... etc. etc. He had been in several relationships but none serious, he was just not the settling down or marrying type. He still believed only in the present, didn't worry about the future, wanted to see as much of the world as he could, still didn't believe in an afterlife).

And then of course on her last evening in London the inevitable happened, the person who had introduced her to her own sexuality in the first place seduced her once again. They had had a lovely dinner, walked the streets of London talking until the wee hours discussing their thoughts and opinions about everything, open with each other about their vulnerabilities, their hopes and disappointments and accomplishments thus far in life. She even shared with him her secret passion for writing which she had discussed with no one. She shared that she would often sit down by the river writing for hours, and indulge in her secret fantasy that someday she would "have a series of popular medical mystery novels" published and become a famous writer, but for now she was practicing by submitting short stories to publishers of women's magazines mainly. Roger would have laughed at her secret ambition and made her feel silly, Andrew thought it was wonderful and encouraged her even offering his help when she got ready for her first novel as he had contacts in the publishing industry. But of course you do, Carolyn thought, but aloud she merely said "Thank-you," amazed that he was actually taking her dream seriously. They opened one last bottle of Dom Perignon back at the hotel and fell easily into each other's arms, not as the beginning of something but rather the conclusion of a long past relationship that had never really had a proper ending. They parted the next morning as two old friends whose relationship had come full circle and they could be comfortable with how it was ending and go back to their real lives. They each voiced the opinion that all in all each of them had made choices in their lives that were right for them individually, he not being the type to settle down and she wanting a family life. She had had a wonderful time, was grateful for having had the chance to connect with Andrew once more and had no thoughts of continuing the relationship any further. She finally felt she had closure on this part of her life. They made the perfunctory gesture of saying "keep in touch" and exchanged contact information as they parted. For her part, Carolyn considered it the end and had no intention of contacting Andrew in the future. She wanted to raise her future children in a stable small college town with Roger, and hoped she hadn't ruined her chances for that.

Carolyn was quite silent on the flight home, reliving her own private adventure while the others relived their golf shots. She was feeling as peaceful as she had in years, and resolved once again to become the wife that Roger wanted and deserved. Of course she realized she would have to tell him about her chance meeting and re-acquaintance with Andrew before the country club crowd did it for her. She would share no details with anyone, least of all Roger.

OCTOBER 1979

She felt the lump when taking a shower, then asked Roger to see if he felt the same thing. "It just feels like a cyst" was his response, "but if you would feel better go see Jeff Mullins and see what he thinks."

The next day she was in Jeff's office. He had remained a good friend and also her physician. "I am certain it is a benign cyst" was Jeff's response, "but let's do some routine lab work and an ultrasound to be sure or we can have a surgeon aspirate it if you are more comfortable with that."

"I want it out" was Carolyn's definitive reply. In her short nursing career she had seen too many people put things off with disastrous results. She had the breast ultrasound that afternoon and was off to see the surgeon the next morning. The ultrasound was negative, however Greg, the surgeon, was unable to aspirate any fluid. His advice was to watch for any change in size and recheck it in four to six months.

"No way" was her firm response, "I am not ignoring this for six months."

The following day she found herself checking in at the Outpatient Surgical Center for a breast biopsy. There were after all advantages of being a physician's wife and so she was able to bypass all the red-tape of booking the minor surgery weeks ahead of time. She told absolutely no one where she was going except for Roger and swore him to secrecy until they knew the results. She would handle this her own way and in her own timeline.

Is this the day my future will be decided she thought as she checked into the center that morning for the biopsy. Despite her being married to Roger, and having worked for Jeff the four years while Roger was finishing his residency and thus she was somewhat known at the hospital, she felt like any other random patient entering those pristine sterile hallways, less than an individual as they checked her in and more just another name on their morning schedule. She hated the impersonal "How are we feeling this morning?" from the nurse checking her in, the impertinence of the "WE" as it was Carolyn not the nurse who was about to have the procedure done. She listened to the happy chatter behind the nursing station desk and thought how could they be so blithe and uncaring while I sit here possibly facing the beginning of the end of my mortal life! She knew she was "losing it" and tried to calm herself down. She sat in the outpatient waiting room in her hospital gown feeling totally vulnerable and alone watching as other patients talked with the close friend or relative accompanying them while they awaited their turn in the operating suite. Had she been foolish to refuse to confide in anyone or let someone come with her? She was sure Terri would have taken the morning off and come with her if she had asked. It helped a bit when Greg himself came out to get her and walked her into the operating suite. The procedure took very little time and after local injection with Novacaine was really not that uncomfortable. The hard part was going to be awaiting the results. Pathology promised they would get back to both Jeff and Greg within 24 hours. She left feeling quite shaken and violated, with her breast colored orange from the Betadine and bandaged heavily. She drove herself home in a daze.

Roger all but ignored her that evening, feeling she was overreacting to a small breast cyst, perhaps looking for some extra attention. Their relationship had seemed to deteriorate even further since her return from Scotland. She had made sure to tell him about meeting Andrew and even about staying with him in London as she was sure that would come out somehow in some conversations at the club. He had really taken it in stride, barely interested in her adventures (of course she hadn't mentioned the last minute sexual encounter which she had "re-lived" in her thoughts several times since her return to the States), and was just more interested in resuming their social obligations and continuing on with their lives. When he found out that Andrew had an office in Alexandria he had even suggested that she invite him to the club for a weekend next time he was in the States so he could meet him and thank him for showing her around. She had no intention of that happening. She and Roger hadn't had sex since her return, mostly her fault for feeling so strange after having slept with Andrew. Their lives were busy and they were just going through the motions and keeping up appearances. But after all, the appearance of a happily married physician was all important to Roger as he felt that benefited his Practice.

He was a dedicated physician enjoying his chosen role in life, and his recreational time at the club was the only outlet he truly seemed to need. He continued to refuse to discuss starting a family as it was always just not quite the right time yet.

She was sitting on the dock overlooking the river the following afternoon watching the birds, the occasional rabbit, deer, squirrels and other wildlife enjoying the sunny fall afternoon. The squirrels were especially busy harvesting and hiding their share of nuts for the winter, which the local farmers would say was a forewarning of a cold winter to come. Her non-hunting retrievers were basking themselves in the sun and occasionally one or the other chased a squirrel up a tree just for the fun of it and then lazily moped back to her own spot on the lawn. They had had a phone line run down to the dock in the early days so Roger would not miss any emergency call that might arise. She had been there the entire day just staring and thinking and waiting for the phone to ring and when it did finally ring she was deathly afraid to pick it up. What course would her life take now if she had breast cancer? Of course discovering it early was a positive, but what did it mean to her desire for children?

"Great news" it was Jeff on the phone. "Biopsy is entirely benign. Just come back in four weeks and we will recheck the breasts and then you can forget this whole incident". She had never felt such overwhelming relief. She called Roger, told him the news and suggested they meet at the club for dinner that evening.

She was ready to celebrate and continue on in her life, vowing once again to be the wife Roger wanted. He was happy to see her wanting to get out again as he felt she had been way too isolated since returning from her trip, perhaps things would return to normal now.

REALITY SINKS IN

The normalcy lasted only a few weeks. When she returned to Jeff's office four weeks later, he had a strange look on his face when he was examining her breasts.

"When was your last menstrual period?"

Though at first she thought it a really strange thing to ask when she was here for a follow-up of her breast biopsy, she quickly realized she hadn't had a period since her return from Scotland in August. She had barely thought about it actually, blaming it on the stress of undergoing the biopsy, the fear of a malignancy. She had recurrent thoughts of guilt regarding Andrew, yet could not make herself feel sorry about the experience. The trip was still a wonderful memory including the time with Andrew even though she knew it was a fleeting and final thing. Yes, she had some guilt, but no regrets. She just figured her hormonal system was a bit off kilter and would return to normal when her life got back into a routine. She also considered for a moment that her mother went through menopause in her early 40's, and she was now 37 so it was possible she was starting to have irregular periods. She thought she better broach the subject of a child with Roger again soon before time passed her by.

"I can't remember exactly but I think around the beginning of August" she replied.

"Let's do a quick urine test here" was Jeff's response and within minutes he was back looking even more perplexed. "Congratulations, looks like you are going to be a mom!"

That is when she fainted. When she came around a few minutes later she was on the couch in Jeff's office with a cold cloth on her head and Terri on a chair by her side. "Wow, that was quite a reaction," she smiled.

"Yes, quite a shock" Carolyn managed to say. "Listen Terri, I need for you and Jeff to not mention anything to Roger right now. I want to find just the right moment to tell him. As you probably know he is not exactly keen on starting a family right now."

"Of course" replied Terri. "I don't want to push you, but could this have anything to do with the time you spent with your former college friend in London?"

Carolyn felt her face flush, she didn't know whether it was anger that Terri would assume she had slept with Andrew, or just guilt in realizing that others who were on the trip may be under that impression as well. They certainly couldn't know that she hadn't slept with Roger since the trip, but how was she supposed to handle telling him of the pregnancy!

"I'm sorry to blurt it out like that." Terri said as she hugged her friend. "You were just so obviously radiant and happy with Andrew and then so quiet on the trip home. Your demeanor shouted 'affair', and now you don't want to rush home and tell your husband after you have waited so long for this to happen?"

"Jeff said he would like to talk with you in the office when you are ready." Terri continued as she helped her up from the couch.

When she entered the office Jeff calmly motioned her toward the chair in his office.

"Look Carolyn, I know this is between you and Roger, but I have known you for a long time both as your former employer as well as your physician, and I consider you a true friend. I also know that Roger had a vasectomy done while in college knowing early on that in his words he was not the 'fatherly type' and that was just not the vision he had for his future. It is unlikely that a vasectomy done that long ago would be reversible even if he did have a change of heart. So, having said that I want you to know that Terri and I are here as friends to help and support you in any way we can with the tough choices you will have in the upcoming weeks."

She could feel herself fading away for the second time…

ONE WEEK LATER

She was once again sitting on the dock staring as the sun set over the west bank of the river, this time with a bottle of Pellegrino sparkling water with lemon rather than wine. This obviously was her place of solace where her soul searching was done and her decisions made. She had some major decisions to make now and needed to confront them soon. She needed someone to talk to but although she could confide in Terri and Jeff, the decisions were hers alone to make and live with the consequences. This was her problem. She watched the retrievers frolic in the river and decided in her next life she was coming back as a dog.

Fortunately Roger was at a week-long hospital board retreat so she had at least a few days to herself to get her thoughts together and basically decide the future course of her life. The overwhelming and most important fact to her was that she was going to be a mom! No one and nothing could change that no matter what course her life took from this point on.

Her first thought was that she owed it to Roger to be completely honest no matter what his reaction. Her second was that she really owed him nothing. He had led her on for years to believe that they would at some point start a family, when that was not really one of his long term goals, and in fact from what Jeff had told her about the vasectomy, not even a possibility. Jenny had told her stories of what a Romeo Roger had been in his undergrad years at U.Va. before he left for Med School at UP. Perhaps that vasectomy was what made him feel so free to sleep around without fear of getting someone pregnant and thus setting his long term goals off track. Did Jenny know about that? She wasn't sure she could even look at him right now let alone confide in him. She had to think fast.

The ironic thing was that superficially her relationship with Roger had gotten better since the breast biopsy and they had even had some friends over for a lovely outdoor dinner by the river since the weather was still unseasonably warm. He was on his way to getting what he had always really wanted, his medical practice was growing, the perfect wife and social hostess, the country club life with its important connections to socially important people and the added advantage of the golf, squash, tennis, and travel opportunities. She was sure that he truly felt he could eventually make her totally happy with that life also. Even the lack of sex hadn't seemed to bother him as long as their social life was going well.

To complicate matters even further Andrew had phoned a couple of weeks ago saying he was going to be in D.C. on business next weekend and could they get together. He had contacted Jenny, remembering her offer to introduce him to some of her clients in Charlottesville next time he was on the East Coast and she had set him up with a room at the club.

"Seriously, I don't want to be a threat to your marriage, I just don't want to lose touch with you again and I would love to meet Roger."

She had reluctantly mentioned the idea to Roger, since she knew that Jenny was bound to bring it up the next time they ran into her, and he had suggested that they arrange to play golf at the Club next weekend with Andrew and Jenny and have dinner on the patio afterwards, and keep it light saying that he would love to meet Andrew.

That was before all this new news…how could she face him now? Should she tell him about the pregnancy? Was it fair to Andrew to disrupt his life with this news? He had already made it clear a family and house in the suburbs was not what his life was all about. She felt like what happened with this pregnancy and who she shared it with was her decision alone, she already had decided she was having this child, so that extended the time she had for deciding who to tell and when.

She spent the rest of the week taking long walks on the wooded trails they had created from the house down to the river, kayaking in the afternoons and eating her salads by the river at night. She really missed her wine and chocolate but she could live without that. She was going to miss this place if she took off on her own to continue her "single mom" role. She knew she could not stay in Charlottesville. She would also miss her faithful retrievers who followed her lovingly and made her feel so peaceful and content, loved, wanted and needed. The river had become the one place she could isolate herself and deal with life's choices. Her secret mystery-writing pastime she had shared with no one but Andrew took place here, and she had even had a couple short stories published in magazines under the her alias, Sarah Church. By the end of the weekend she had come up with her plan. It wasn't perfect, it was far from honest as she would be lying to both Roger and Andrew, but it was the best she could do and she was going to learn to live with it. She would lay the ground work next weekend while Andrew was in town, she had a few weeks before Roger would become suspicious and in the meantime she would lay out her plan hopefully with Andrew's help. Her only doubt was if she could pull it off in a way both men would believe her.

She sat and watched a huge red-crested pileated woodpecker at work drilling a perfectly round hole in a dying tree on the river bank in search of insects while letting out his distinct loud piercing call. Nature was truly amazing. If only she was a more knowledgeable survivalist perhaps she would move out west, maybe in the wilderness areas of northern Arizona, have the baby and live off the land, maybe more plausibly to a Caribbean or South Pacific island and work in a remote hospital. But of course those romantic fantasies were unrealistic in so many ways, and were definitely not THE plan. She allowed herself to laugh silently for the first time in weeks. After all, she had no clue how to live without modern conveniences let alone survive and bring up a child that way.

As Roger returned home and Andrew's weekend visit got closer she began wavering in her decision. She wondered if she should be honest with him, after all shouldn't she let him know that he was about to be a father? That way if his reaction was negative she would at least not have to carry the guilt of not having given him the option to decide what his role in the child's life should or would be. Or on the other hand should she take the chance of his feeling obligated to support her either monetarily or feel that he should be with her and support her through the pregnancy. She knew she did not want either of those reactions. If she were honest with herself she wanted to relieve herself of the guilt of not having told him and given him options, and yet hoped that he would just somehow turn around and say, "sorry, your problem" and perhaps disappear as he had done back in their college days. Then the child would be all hers. The stark reality however was that she needed Andrew's help and his worldly connections to make her plan work. She felt she instinctively would know the best course after seeing him this weekend. Interestingly she was not so worried about what Roger's reaction to her disappearance would be. She had known Jenny long enough to know that if she were out of the picture, Jenny would step right in there to comfort Roger. It was to Jenny's credit that she hadn't tried to worm her way back into Roger's life the moment he had moved back to Charlottesville. She was worried how she could carry off the next few weeks living with Roger without revealing the anger she felt regarding his deceit all these years. Of course her little fling with Andrew and thus her present situation didn't leave her totally void of any wrongdoing in their marriage either.

The one person she knew she could confide in was Terri. She and Jeff already knew of the pregnancy and the suspected father, and she knew they would help her in whatever future plan she decided upon.

The weekend with Andrew went better than she had imagined it could. Roger had returned from his meeting on Friday and suggested they dine at the 19th Hole with Jenny to firm up the weekend plan. Andrew would be arriving early Saturday morning. That was fine with Carolyn as it left no "alone time" for she and Roger before the busy weekend plans began.

The four of them met for golf mid-morning on Saturday. Roger and Andrew actually were about the same handicap and quickly fell into a friendly competitive game. She and Jenny rode together and enjoyed the outing (or at least Jenny did…). Carolyn's thoughts were centered on the conversation she had to have with Andrew before he left town. She had still not decided whether that conversation would include the 'fatherhood issue' or not.

"Look at this woman! Roger what have you done with this totally non-athletic woman I knew in college?" Andrew remarked as Carolyn's shot on the short par three landed just a few feet from a hole in one. The friendly banter continued throughout the afternoon. So much for all the golf pros' and sports psychologists' advice to just keep your mind on each shot and put aside all other thoughts while on the course. Carolyn was following some of the golf mantra such as not to over-try once on the course and to let your golf muscle memory take over, just aim at the target with a nice relaxed swing.

That evening the four of them dined on the club's outside patio. When Roger went off to talk to some of his friends and Jenny went to "powder her nose" she and Andrew were finally alone for a few minutes and she started to lay her plans.

"Roger is great" Andrew said sincerely. "You made a good choice Carolyn, this seems like the good life and I am happy for you. As for me I would never have been happy settling down to this as I am much too restless, so it looks like our lives took the right turns after all". Andrew did not know it, but that statement sealed Carolyn's decision.

"Andrew, I need a big favor from you and I obviously don't have time to discuss it right now. Things are not as they seem on the surface. Do you think there is any chance you and I could meet tomorrow before you return to D.C. and places beyond?" She tried to sound casual about it but he could hear the seriousness in her voice and see the concern in her eyes.

"As a matter of fact I have told Jenny that I would accompany her to a house party tomorrow evening so I won't be leaving until Monday morning. She is an amazing woman, quite fun actually and is going to introduce me to some of the more important business people in Charlottesville which might come in handy in the future, you never know. I could meet you for an hour or so before leaving town Monday morning if that works for you. You have certainly peaked my curiosity."

"That would be perfect. Meet me at my house Monday around 10 a.m... I will call you with directions. Oh, and please don't mention anything to Jenny."

Carolyn slept well that night, her plan was now in place, her decision made. Now she just needed Andrew to help her implement it in the quickest way possible.

MONDAY MORNING

"So basically you are asking me to help you disappear?"

Andrew had arrived as promised around 10 a.m. and she met him at the door with a picnic basket saying "I want to show you my favorite spot in the whole wide world." They walked through the trails to the river and sat on the dock watching the wild life, listening to the babble of the water flowing over the rocks as she told him of her plight. The dogs followed as always.

She continued on with her story as they sipped their tea, "You know the truly weird thing about all this is that the only thing I will really miss is the river and the dogs. This has been my haven for the past ten years away from all the superficiality of my country club life. Roger has been a good provider, but he does not want a family and would not want this child. I know that he would want me to have an abortion which I just cannot do." What she did not tell Andrew was that the reality of all this was that he was the father of her child, which she was sure he would not want to hear nor would he handle the situation any better than Roger. She also did not tell him of her recent discovery of Roger's previous vasectomy. No, she had decided this was her decision and her responsibility and as she daily got more and more used to the idea she was feeling more and more of a connection with the tiny person growing within her and looking forward to dedicating her life to raising him or her.

"Suppose I could find a way to help you disappear.......what are you going to tell Roger and how are you going to support the child? Have you really thought all this through? You are making a momentous life changing decision in a moment of shock at your situation. Also are you being fair to Roger in not letting him have his say regarding the baby?"

"Andrew, you are the only person I can turn to. Believe me my decision is made and though I know I will be hurting Roger somewhat by leaving him I also know the community and his friends will rally around him and he will truly be fine." She wholeheartedly believed this statement.

She continued, taking a deep breath and looking Andrew squarely in the eyes, "As for letting Roger be part of this decision, the baby is not his."

She waited for Andrew's reaction, once again wondering if he would put the timeline together but was just met by a blank stare on his part. He never even asked or seemed interested in who the father was if not Roger.

"As for how to support myself and my child in the future, that will come. I can't plan my whole life strategy at this point. I do have a nursing degree which I can turn back to in order to make a living eventually and I have been trying to build a writing career, but what I first need is your help over the upcoming year. I need to disappear without a trace and somehow I figured with your connections around the world you could make that possible. I also need a good Obstetrician and a place for my child to be born. Please help me."

Andrew unbelievably replied immediately with no judgment in his voice nor any hint of understanding the underlying truth regarding the baby.

"Carolyn, we have a very remote history together but I truly feel our lives have connected together again for some reason, let me see what I can come up with but it will take a few weeks." Seeing the look on her face he quickly continued "Now don't look at me like that, I am not saying I believe in fate or a higher being managing our lives or any of that. I have not changed that much since college, I still believe that this earth and this life is all there is and nothing more. I also believe each one of us has to do what we feel we must with our lives and if this is what you are sure you want I will try and help you." No questions asked, he was just going to help her and then probably gleefully get back to his own life. This attitude made her very grateful to him and at the same time even more determined in her solitary plan.

They parted with the idea that he would call within a week with a tentative plan and she in the meantime would decide how to handle her departure. How to handle being alone with Roger for the next couple of weeks would be a problem. She thought of perhaps a shopping trip to D.C. with Terri for a few days might solve some of that issue and also give she and Terri a chance to talk. She decided she would call her in the morning.

PLANNING FOR THE IMMEDIATE FUTURE

"So the plan is this" Carolyn continued. Terri had been unable to take enough time off from the office for the shopping trip to D.C., and they had decided to spend Wednesday, Terri's day off with a nice fall hike by the river followed by a picnic lunch. It was a perfect fall day, breezy but still in the 60's, and the trails were beginning to be covered with bright orange, yellow and red leaves. The dogs accompanied them on their walk and delighted in trying to catch the falling leaves, and crunch on the acorns that were scattered on the ground. Terri and Jeff were still the only ones who shared the knowledge of her pregnancy other than Andrew. Difference was that they knew the child was Andrew's.

As she began spreading the cheese, fresh bread, fruit, cider out on the blanket for lunch, Carolyn explained that she needed both she and Jeff to continue in complete secrecy about the pregnancy as she still didn't know what her plans would be after the child was born, she would have to face that later. In the meantime she explained that she knew Roger would have a hard time with her leaving, not so much because of his closeness with her but because of the impact on his status in the community and having to face his friends and the fact that his wife and he were undergoing a trial separation, which she had decided would be the official statement to the country club set. Carolyn was still convinced that in the long run he would be able to maintain the things most important to him, his status in the community, his medical practice, his recreational sports life at the club. He would need the public and private support though especially from Terri and Jeff to get him through handling the initial disappearance. She knew that Roger as well as the entire community would think she had run off with Andrew, as the story of the golf trip mystery man would undoubtedly be told over and over again. That fact made it very important that she not run away to London where Andrew was living, much too easy to trace the connection that way.

She disclosed her plan to Terri as they munched on their feast. She planned to tell Roger she needed a period of time to herself to think about what she wanted for the rest of her life. That he had been a good husband and provider but she felt they were drifting apart, leading almost separate superficial lives, and that perhaps they needed to face that fact before it was too late for either of them to pursue another path. She suggested he tell people they were trying a trial separation and she was off traveling and seeing the world, sort of a suburban housewife's sabbatical. It made her seem harsh and cold but she really didn't care what the social crowd thought of her. Imagine what they would think if they knew the truth. She promised Terri that she would keep in touch with she and Jeff and let them know where her life was headed and about her future decisions regarding the baby. She had decided not to tell Roger that she knew about the vasectomy as that would involve telling him how she had found out about it…that was best left unspoken.

For the immediate future she had withdrawn a hefty amount from their joint savings account, which was easily done and she handled the family finances and Roger oversaw their stock portfolio. She then had Andrew place the funds in a bank in Barcelona for her under her writing alias of Sarah Church, leaving Roger most of their money and all of their other assets. Andrew had arranged for her to meet with a Gynecologist in Barcelona in a couple of weeks, and then had gotten her a temporary assignment writing travel pieces about the shore excursions offered on an Italian Cruise ship with a calm Mediterranean route where she would have the ship's doctor to consult for any emergency medical needs. She in turn had promised to check in with her OB/GYN in Barcelona on her one week off from the ship every six weeks. Her baby would be delivered in Spain. She figured she had enough money to last her about a year so the travel writing job would be wonderful and she also planned to work on completing her first mystery novel which had been floating around in her head before all these later developments in her life. Relocating to London to be near Andrew was out of the question as no doubt he would be the first person Roger would suspect of helping her. Andrew needed to have complete deniability. And that was how "Sarah Church" would become a real person instead of the name she had been using thus far for her short stories, and how all traces of "Carolyn Blackstone" would disappear. Andrew had also arranged all the necessary paper work and documents for her new life ...in her new name of course. Wow, she had imagined that he had lots of "connections" through his business and travel over the past years but didn't know just how varied those connections were, and the more she thought about it knew she knew that she didn't really want to know the details! She however selfishly was willing to take advantage of his connections. She was truly starting a new life and was actually getting very excited about it and looking forward to the year ahead for the first time in a long time with a sense of adventure and of course the anticipation of becoming a mother. She knew her Catholic conscience would bother her in the deep darkness of some long nights, but she was determined to plunge forward with a positive attitude and start a new life for herself and her unborn child. Now she just had to get through the motions of a normal life here in Charlottesville until 'Sarah Church' departed for Spain via Florida then Frankfort, Germany. She would spend a few days in Germany and change airlines just to make any trail even harder to follow.

Carolyn was looking at her in disbelief. "Have you even considered that you have never even flown on your own before and now you are taking on this elaborate complicated journey? Not to mention as far as I know you speak neither German nor Spanish!"

"I know, and 6 months ago those are exactly the things that would have entered my mind when Andrew introduced his plan. But now I am about to become a mother and it's about time to start taking charge of my own life before I begin taking care of a child."

"You could just divorce Roger, tell Andrew about the baby, and either settle with him in London, or even better just stay here and raise the baby where you have friends to support you. Believe me in this town your situation will be old news quickly whenever the next "club scandal" hits, as you know it always does." Terri said with a slight smirk.

"Who knows, perhaps someday I shall return here, but for now this is the plan. I really need these next 6 months or so alone with my thoughts, to 'plan the rest of my life' as the saying goes." She gave Terri a hug and with tears in her eyes told her this would not be the last time they saw each other no matter where her decisions led her.

TWO WEEKS LATER

The traffic on I-95 was not all that bad. Andrew had arranged for a rental car in his name and she took a cab to the rental agency. She had picked a Wednesday mid-morning departure knowing Roger would be at the club playing with his regular foursome weather permitting and on the off chance it rained he would be on the squash court or at the gym, he was entirely predictable never leaving time for boredom, his worst fear. She had never known him to spend his mid-week day off at home. She left a note on the mantle asking that he not try to contact her nor trace her whereabouts. She had not however told him the exact timing of her departure as she felt they had re-hashed her "year-off" plans enough and a prolonged goodbye would just make things harder.

She pulled into the Potomac Mills Shopping Center precisely at one o'clock. Andrew was waiting in a small booth by the window of the restaurant where they had chosen to meet. He handed her a small black case filled with documents. She had left the planning of her adventure in his capable hands.

"To new beginnings," he smiled easily as she sat down.

Once her decision had been made Andrew had taken over. The first folder he handed her contained one-way train tickets from Lorton, Virginia, to Sanford, Florida, for Sarah Church. Though traveling on the auto-train, she would not have an auto. It was just convenient in that it was a direct route with no in-between stops, and of course no one would think of checking for her on an auto-train, once they found her rental car had been returned then the airport would be the next logical place to look if they wanted to trace her whereabouts. He had arranged for someone to pick her up at the restaurant, drop her off at the train station and drive the car back to the local rental agency. One-way car rental was very efficient. If somehow ever started looking for her hopefully her trail would end here. Looking at the name on the ticket she felt a twinge of excitement in spite of the problems she knew would lie ahead.

The second folder contained a new passport and credit cards for Sarah Church. She would need ID to get onto the train.

"I have arranged for a friend to pick you up tomorrow at Sanford and drive you to the Jacksonville Airport, from there you will fly to Barcelona via Atlanta. Someone will meet you in Barcelona and get you settled in. I will meet you there in a few days via London." Her heart fluttered as she thanked him, gave him a quick hug and took off with her driver.

At the train station Carolyn looked about the large waiting area for an isolated seat, she found one in an enclosed picnic area outside the front entrance. She had an hour before the boarding the train and she was exhausted already. She carried only one rolling suitcase, and Andrew would bring the larger one with him when they met in Barcelona. She was looking for a seat where she wouldn't get trapped into talking to anyone. Andrew had arranged for a sleeper cabin so she could relax, sort through her thoughts, and begin immersing herself in life as Sarah Church. Carolyn Blackstone was about to disappear forever.

FIRST VOYAGE
DECEMBER 1979

"Sarah, my name is Mark Blanchard and I am a friend of Andrew's. I am also the ship's cruise director on board and I understand you will be joining us for our next voyage starting in a few days." Wow. It was really happening! She felt a twinge of excitement upon hearing the voice at the other end of the line. She had been expecting this call, yet hearing an actual voice made her newest venture a reality.

She was still having a hard time adjusting to her new name. It had been a crazy month with so much happening but here she was now into her fourth month of pregnancy and feeling absolutely wonderful. Andrew had helped get her set up in a small flat on the outskirts of Barcelona two blocks from the beach and not far from the harbor where the cruise ships docked. She was to pay for her own cabin for the first two week voyage and would submit her travel articles to the cruise line office upon the ship's return to Barcelona and go from there. If the marketing department liked the articles, she would sail a few more times with them and do some more in-depth writing about the ports the ship visited, before the baby was born and see what happened from there. She was very excited about the opportunity and did not see where the pregnancy would interfere at all, at least not unless she got seasick. She had as promised met with an English speaking Gynecologist and his nurse practitioner and would keep up her monthly prenatal care and deliver in Barcelona when the time arrived....EDC sometime in May...this was the beginning of December. She had less than 5 months to prove to the cruise company that she really could be an asset to them as an independent travel writer. She would research the Mediterranean ports to begin with and then perhaps after the baby was born hopefully venture out into other geographic areas, continuing to plow on with the first of what she hoped would be her mystery series featuring her nurse heroine. Yes, she was getting the travel bug back that she and Andrew had talked about oh so long ago in their college years. Only this time although Andrew had proved to be a good friend in helping her in her present situation he would not be the permanent life companion she had once envisioned. She was grateful (and amazed) at all his "connections" that he had pulled together to help her create a new life, but all the more convinced each time they were together that he would not be a great father nor did she think he would even want to know there was that possibility. She did not make that decision lightly but never doubted that it was the right one for him, the child and herself. Of course she still hadn't decided who would care for the child while she continued on with her writing and traveling as a necessity of supporting herself and her son or daughter as a single mother. As an infant of course she could bring the child with her on her travels, but once he/she needed more structure and schooling then what... one problem at a time became her motto. In her spare time she was studying Spanish from tapes and planning to take on Italian next. She was thoroughly embarrassed by the fact that most Europeans spoke at least three major languages, while most Americans spoke only their own native English.

The voice on the other end had a surreal quality to it. "Hello Mark, I have been expecting your call. I understand the ship docks tonight and is here for two days prior to re-sailing and that perhaps I could get to visit and get somewhat of a sneak peek?"

"Of course" came the friendly reply. "Today they will be quite busy with disembarking the current passengers and cleaning up and re-setting up the ship. Usually our turn- around time is quick but this is a scheduled two day maintenance break, so I could show you around the ship tomorrow if you like. You could even have your choice of the un-booked cabins for your first voyage. You may want to come aboard early on Friday before the mayhem begins with the passenger arrivals that afternoon, you know how that is." He said this with a chuckle as if she would know exactly what he meant. Had Andrew failed to mention that she had never even seen a cruise ship up close Carolyn wondered with a smirk?

And so Friday morning found her standing in front of the huge embarkation building waiting for Mark, whom she only knew from a description on the phone. She stared at the huge ship in front of her. Since she had only actually seen cruise ships in travel brochures and ads on TV…never up close and personal… this one looked huge. She had read up a bit and the "Columbus" as she was called, had a capacity of 1100 passengers in addition to a sizeable crew which amounted to something like one employee for every 20 passengers. She had her preconceived ideas from the brochure of what it would be like inside but couldn't wait for her private tour. Hopefully Mark had remembered he promised to meet her here at 9 this morning. Her misgivings and doubt were soon allayed as she heard his pleasant voice from behind her.

"She is a beauty isn't she?"

"Mark, I presume" Carolyn extended her hand to meet his outstretched arm. "Thank you so much for suggesting this way of easing into my journey. I have a feeling Andrew hasn't told you that I have never even stepped aboard a sailboat no less a huge vessel such as this."

"Well, both vessels sail but the comparison definitely stops there." He chided her.

"Of course I was not comparing the vessels nor the sailing experience, just letting you know my sea travels have been extremely limited up to this point, in fact nonexistent would be a more accurate description. I plan to correct that in the future."

She could not help being surprised at how young Mark Blanchard was and yes, how very attractive. She had kind of pictured an older person being the director of a cruise ship, and had not asked any questions when Andrew made these arrangements. She wondered how much Andrew had told him about her situation. How much had he told the rest of the ship's staff about her? She assumed and hoped he had told them only that she was a writer, and a pregnant one at that as her physical condition would be hard to conceal for very much longer. Did they think she was single, divorced, widowed?

"Well, are you ready to step aboard?" Mark's pleasant calm voice brought her out of her thoughts and back to the present.

Somehow "stepping aboard" meant entering the huge terminal, going through security checks, up an escalator to the second floor which had a clear plexiglass entry tube that extended to the fifth deck of the ship, which in turn opened into the ship's main lobby. Her understanding from the brochure was that the lower decks contained sleeping quarters, plus the two main dining rooms at each end of one of the lower decks as the stability there was better if the seas got rough. She really didn't want to think about that. Below the passenger rooms were the crew's quarters and the infirmary. Also the "theater" was set on one of the lower decks for the same stability factors since they put on shows which involved dancing, magic acts etc for which they needed the stage to be as steady as possible during rough weather.

"Shall we start at the top?" Mark guided her into a glass elevator in the center of the atrium in the main lobby where they rose up to the highest deck. Upon leaving the elevator they were faced with the large glass double doors entering into the luxury spa and exercise room. The exercise bikes and treadmills pointed out toward the front of the ship, with the weight lifting equipment more toward the center of the room. Instead of watching TV while on the bikes as in the gyms back home, you would be staring out at the sea as the ship made its path through the water. She wasn't quite sure yet if this was a frightening or comforting thought. In the inner rooms were the saunas, steam rooms, massage tables with their heating stones, areas set up for facials, nails, hair grooming etc etc., all of the luxury and pampering any spa could offer. Heading toward the middle of the ship they crossed beside the outdoor pools, hot tubs, outdoor grill and on toward the back of the ship. There was even an outdoor movie screen reminiscent of drive-in movie. Amazing! Then on to the infamous 24 hour dining area advertised in all cruise brochures. This would consist of buffet stations of all nationalities of food from 7 a.m. through 9 p.m., outside those hours the self-serve stations for juice, coffee, ice cream and snacks would stay open 24 hours. At midnight they would serve the infamous chocolate buffet on selected evenings. She remembered the stories people would tell of how much weight they had gained on their cruises and vowed to not let that happen to her, she would be gaining enough weight for a very different reason. The pregnancy weight would be welcomed and that would be enough pounds to put on for one cruise. Mark assured her if she wanted more of a "sit down and be served meal" there were 4 additional restaurants on board serving French, Italian, Asian or Moroccan food, and of course the two main dining rooms one at each end of the ship, all on the lower decks. She resolved to restrain herself, after all she had an obligation to the little one inside her to eat healthily despite all the temptations. She would be concentrating on her writing and language skills on this voyage so that she could land a real job as a travel writer when this six month trial phase was over. She also needed the quiet time alone to decide what would happen after the baby was born… She had only thus far allowed herself to get to the birth date, she now had but a few solitary months to plan her future and that of her unborn child. She could feel some rumblings already which she didn't know if they were actual fetal movements or just "gas" as some people said occurred at this stage. The one thing she knew for certain was that Andrew would never know that this child was his. He had made it perfectly clear he was not the "family man" type and she did not want to change that with any pressure on her part. He was sweet to help her and was asking little about her plans, he had agreed to help her out with her disappearance, setting her up with living quarters and a job writing, having her child solo, and then it was up to her after that. She wondered if he was sorry they had ever gotten reacquainted last summer. He could never have foreseen getting this involved in her life once again she was sure.

The one person she was keeping up with as promised was Terri. To her she could reveal all her true feelings. Terri in turn was providing unconditional support through her letters, with promises to visit when it got closer to delivery time. She was her one true friend, she had broken contact with all of her country club "acquaintances" she had made over the years in Virginia and oddly missed none of them, nor did she miss the suburban country club life she had lived. "Carolyn" was truly in the past, her golf adventures and sports goals and aspirations far behind her. It now all seemed a rather frivolous life looking back on it. Terri's last letter had informed her that Jenny was doing her best to comfort Roger, which Carolyn was sure she was! Both of them probably absolutely certain that she had run off with her college sweetheart, though neither having any inkling of the pregnancy. Carolyn also knew from Andrew, always the business man opportunist, that he was keeping in touch with Jenny and her "contacts" and denying any knowledge of Carolyn's whereabouts. She was sure Jenny was trying to trip him up on his stories, just as he was trying to use her contacts to benefit his career and convince everyone he had nothing to do with this disappearing act. They were a good match for each other and she just had to trust that Andrew would not give away anything. She was actually enjoying the fact that she had both Terri and Andrew letting her know what was happening in her former town. She was sure they were both also trying to shelter her from all the ugly gossip. It was hard to believe that just six months ago her only plan was getting ready for the Country Club "A" women's golf team! Wow! How quickly fate steps in and changes the status quo, here she was now planning a Mediterranean cruise, not to mention the birth of her first child.

She followed Mark through the upper decks, the library, the more expensive cabins, indoor movie theater, shops. It was like being in a huge resort hotel, except that she would be traveling while sleeping in her own comfy room at night. No airline hassle, no packing/unpacking. Not many of the staff were on board as they were enjoying a free day on shore before sailing off to what to them were very familiar ports as they traveled this route every 15 to 21 days over and over during their six month tour on duty, then had six weeks off. The cleaning staff however were busy at work shining all the glass, hand-railings, mopping floors and making sure the ship looked its very best and made a good first impression on passengers arriving on Friday. Most of the wait staff, room stewards etc. were from poor areas and small countries or islands and the money they made was very good compared to what they could have made on land in their homelands. However most also had families at home and very much looked forward to getting home for their six weeks off once the novelty of "seeing the world" wore off. They worked hard while at sea.

"Would you like to see the empty cabins that are available to you?"

"Oh yes." She felt like she was in a fairy land. She had seen some sample cabins on each of the decks and the most she hoped for was that one of available cabins would have at least a window she could open. She didn't know if she could survive being closed into one of the inner cabins with no outdoor air. Might have to sleep on one of the outdoor decks if that is to be my fate, she thought to herself and simply use the cabin for showering and storing her clothes.

To her utmost surprise and delight Mark headed toward an upper deck to show her a cabin that faced the back of the ship but had a balcony! She immediately said this would be perfect.

"I must be honest with you. The cabins mid ship are steadier in a storm although the available ones don't have balconies, but if we hit a patch of bad weather this location could possibly get a little rocky."

"No problem" she replied as she secretly thought again she would just go to a public area mid ship in case of a storm. There was no way she would stay alone in her closed cabin by herself during a storm no matter what time of night or day it was. She vowed she would keep a close eye on the weather forecasts and probably sleep in her clothes just in case a storm were to arrive quickly. Ha, she thought to herself, and what makes you think you can become a seasoned traveler so quickly. She also wondered if his concern about her getting seasick was related to his knowledge of her pregnant state, she secretly hoped that Andrew had paved the way for her and told at least the upper staff of her present condition as she would hate for it to be a surprise, and she was definitely planning on this as a source of income until at least the beginning of her 8th or 9th month.

As they headed back down to the main lobby to register her in the cabin she had chosen, Mark asked quietly, "And would you like to see our little infirmary where anything medical can be handled 24/7?" Hmm, what a polite way of acknowledging that yes, he did know of her "condition." She replied that of course she would, while thinking to herself that hopefully she would not be spending any time there during the upcoming voyages.

"This is really quite impressive" Carolyn remarked as he showed her the well-stocked emergency department. "It must be very comforting for the passengers to know all this is here."

"Andrew told me that you trained as a nurse in college. Did you work at all professionally after graduating?"

This seemed as good a time as any to clear the air and find out exactly what Andrew had told Mark and the rest of the staff about her. She explained that she had worked for a few years for a Family Practice physician (true) after graduating. Then she discovered her true passion for writing and decided to try her hand at that. When she found herself unexpectedly pregnant as a result of a short-term relationship, her life had once again taken an unexpected turn (sort of true), and that she was planning to have this child on her own (true). She didn't want any details available that he could trace either back to her college years nor her marriage and life in Virginia.

As they were starting to leave the infirmary and go back up to the atrium, a young blonde woman who looked to be in her mid 20's entered.

"Mark, I didn't expect to see you here today. I am just doing some last minute inventory before leaving for the afternoon, can I do anything for you? " She smiled.

Mark turned to the young woman, "Sasha, this is Sarah Church. She is going to be onboard with us this voyage doing some travel articles on our ship and the various ports. Sarah, this is Sasha, our nurse on the Columbus, she pretty much runs this clinic, though Dr. Keeler thinks he does." The three of them exchanged pleasantries with promises to have lunch or dinner together over the next few days at sea. It was the perfect way to end any further discussion into Carolyn's circumstances.

They ended the tour with Mark giving her a map of the ship and telling her she could come aboard anytime. The ship would be sailing at 4 p.m. the following day. She decided to have one last night in Barcelona and board early Friday morning. She thanked Mark for his tour and spent some time on her own finding her way around the ship. She returned once more to the cabin that would be her home-base for the next few weeks. She felt excitement and a sense that all would work out for the best in the future. It just had to.

MAJOR CHANGES

When she returned to the hotel she was both shocked and pleased to find Andrew in the lobby.

"I can't have you depart on your first voyage without a proper send-off" he said with a huge grin. "I have reservations at the best local tapas place in Barcelona for 9:30 this evening."

A few hours later after she had gotten her things organized for the morning departure, Mark had arranged for someone from the ship to pick her up at 9 a.m., there she was sitting opposite the man she once had loved, the unsuspecting father of her unborn child, with feelings that she just could not bring to the surface. He was so happy, so carefree, so willing to help in her awkward situation as a close old friend who she knew was genuinely concerned with her welfare and her decisions and willing to support whatever she chose to do. He of course she realized also believed that she was running away from her former life, her husband and what he understood to be her recent lover's baby.

After dispensing with all the niceties and small talk, and a few glasses of Sangria on Andrew's part, they finally got down to really talking.

"I don't want to push this issue Carolyn, you know I will continue to support you in anything you decide for your own future, but as a male I must wonder what the father of your child is thinking at this moment.

Are you in touch at all? Does he know you are planning to raise this child without him?"

Carolyn hadn't prepared for this moment, but thought okay, let's see where this conversation leads us.

"Andrew, my relationship with my soon-to-be born child's father was short-lived, and although I once cared deeply for him in the past, he is not the family-man type, our relationship is over, and I do not want to trap him into becoming a father when that clearly is not how he envisions his life unfolding."

Andrew's face had turned white. Had he figured that perhaps the child could be his? Had he started counting the months since that fateful moment in his London apartment? She only hoped not, as she could see it was not a pleasant look but a very scared look that she was seeing across the table at this moment. If Carolyn had had a moment's doubt about opening up and telling Andrew the entire truth, that look again confirmed the course she now knew she would continue to follow.

She replied in an even voice, "I hope you won't think too badly of me Andrew. My marriage had not been good of late, Roger and I have drifted apart and our goals and values are just not the same anymore. I don't know if Roger has ever been unfaithful to me, I kind of doubt it as he has a very full life with his medical practice and his country club activities. He seems to desire nothing more than that. I allowed myself to stray as I guess I have been quite lonely and I found someone I had known well and who I really could talk to." Andrew was turning paler as she spoke.

"It was someone whom I had known for many years as a friend, and obviously one thing led to another and voila! Here I am with child." She tried to make light of it and let Andrew off the hook. "Once we had slept together as the euphemism goes, we both knew it was just an escape and would solve nothing and we both again went our separate ways, he back to his family, and well me....here I am. I haven't seen him since, he has no idea regarding the pregnancy and will just think like everyone else at the club does that I am just selfishly off to travel and see the world while my saintly husband continues saving people's lives." It was amazing how the untruths just poured out of her with ease, perhaps the would-be writer in her was taking over she thought glibly.

The color had come back into Andrew's cheeks as he now let himself believe that at least he was sure he had nothing to do with this latest problem except that he was helping out an old friend. He had just had to be sure. He could now be more open and honest with her.

"How can you be sure the baby is not Roger's?" was the next question out of Andrew's mouth. She then explained the two things that made her certain, one that she had not had sex with Roger in quite a long time, and two that she knew about the vasectomy that he had had in college. She explained how she had found out about this accidentally from Jeff Mullins.

A strange look came over Andrew's face once again. "I was wondering if you knew" was all he said. He then went on to say that he had been wanting to have this conversation and not have secrets from each other.

He wanted them to be true friends, completely honest with each other. He didn't want her to think he was doing anything behind her back. Seeing her puzzled look, he went on to explain.

"To be perfectly honest Carolyn, which I want us to be with each other, I needed you to tell me that you knew for sure that the baby was not Roger's." Now it was she who had the puzzled look on her face. Was she reaching the wrong conclusions here, had he after all done the math and realized he could be the father? If so he must also realize it was much too late to "fix the situation."

"Remember that weekend I spent with Jenny in Charlottesville before you told me about your pregnancy? Andrew continued, while Carolyn hung on every word.

"We got to talking about you, the golf trip where we re-met, etc. and after a few drinks Jenny told me that one of the reasons she was so intent on getting you to go on that trip was so that you would forget about the 'having a family' thing and center more on having a fun life filled with golf, friends, parties, travel and in her mind all the things that made life worth living."

He went on to say that Jenny told him that Roger had had a vasectomy in college as he knew he never wanted a family and that it was breaking her heart to see you believing that that was somehow something Roger was just "putting off" not something that she knew he had completely ruled out long ago. "She said that Roger truly loved you and thought he could eventually make you happy even without a family."

"So you see when you told me you were pregnant I knew before you even told me about your affair, that the baby was not Roger's but didn't feel it was my place to confront you with that, I felt that was your business and you would tell me about the father if you wanted to. My job was just to help you as a friend plan the future you wanted for yourself and the child."

"However still I must ask, don't you think that the person who did father this child has a right to know you are carrying his baby so he can make his own decisions?"

Now it was Carolyn's turn to be completely stunned. How could Andrew not know that the timing so made it possible that that man was him! Since he had known about Roger's sterility had he also been suspecting/dreading that he might be the father and was just giving her time to drop that little tidbit of information? Was he still really waiting to hear the "real truth" from her lips? Was this what his conversation about wanting them to be "completely honest with each other" really about? Yet at the same time she could see the immense relief in his face that she had confessed to an affair with an old friend who in his mind was obviously not him.

"No" she replied. "This person is also very settled and happy with his own life and it would ruin his happiness, not enhance it. This is my child and my decision." Partial truth, but she was sure this time that she saw true belief and relief on Andrew's face.

The evening went back to small talk, with Andrew returning her to her hotel and making her promise to let him know how things were going. She could clearly see how content he was to have had this discussion.

"I will not be around when the ship returns from your first voyage as my travel schedule is rather tight the next few months. However I expect constant updates and of course I am only a phone call away if any trouble arises." He said as he walked her into the lobby.

With that sentence she knew their lives once again were taking different paths. The relief in the air and on his face to be once again entirely on his own was palpable.

LIFE AS "SARAH CHURCH" NOVEMBER 1979 TO APRIL 1980 CRUISING THE MEDITERRANEAN SEA

Her first sailing was as a pregnant single woman leaving from Barcelona and was amazing, truly opening her eyes to different cultures and sparking her interest in travel once again. She had arrived at the dock the morning after her dinner with Andrew feeling that her new life was about to begin, completely on her own and that was now fine with her. As she settled in, Mark arrived and insisted on taking her around and introducing her to the people who would be most important and helpful to her on her voyage, beginning with re-introducing Sasha. He reassured her that if he were not available and she needed anything, pregnancy questions answered, minor health issues etc., information about upcoming ports or anything related to the cruise ship itself that she could trust Sasha completely. As it turned out, Sasha became a close friend, confidante, and an amazing source of strength for Carolyn as the months leading up to her delivery date came closer. Carolyn was to find out as their friendship progressed, that Sasha had been adopted from a Russian orphanage by an American couple from New Jersey.

Carolyn's first challenge was to remember that she was now "Sarah Church." That was quite confusing for her in the beginning and she often stammered when introducing herself or was being introduced as "Sarah."

During that first cruise as Sarah Church the travel writer, she began to formulate a plan that she could live with, and the nights alone at sea on her balcony became almost as comforting, perhaps more comforting, than her life as Carolyn Blackstone the golf-and-tennis country club wife had been. As she had expected, what she most missed was her river haven and her dogs. She would sit on the decks alone at night contemplating the stars and the realities and meaning of life. She began reading philosophy books from the ship's library.

Mark became her go-to expert regarding the cruising world and the ports they visited. He also became a true friend. On that first cruise, when he could manage the time off from the ship he offered to take her on a more personal tour of the ports they visited. That is when it was possible, such as in Rome, Athens and Istanbul. In the ports where it was not quite as safe, since it was most of the time mandatory to see the sites with a certified tour guide and accompanying security guard such as in Cairo and Alexandria, they just accompanied the more formal tour groups and then inched off a bit on their own while staying within the confines of the group. She would never forget her first glimpse of the pyramids with Mark sitting beside her on the tour bus.

"Wow" was all she could lamely manage to say as they got closer and she could see the Giza pyramids begin to appear out the right-side window of the bus.

"I never tire of seeing the wonder in someone's eyes as they view that site for the first time. No matter how much we read or how many documentaries we see, I don't think we can really understand how these people accomplished such a feat with the knowledge and tools available to them at that time in history. That becomes even more true as you actually see them up close." Mark said, and he looked genuinely elated himself to be able to share her wonder.

She couldn't help remember how much Roger hated to travel, saying "Looks just like the pictures, videos etc. you have seen a thousand times in books and magazines" on the few adventures they had taken together. "You might as well stay home in the comfort of your own home and read about them or watch a travelogue video now-a-days."

Mark on the other hand began sharing all kinds of tiny bits of information he had collected on these tours over the years. "See those round-looking shapes up on poles with several holes in them surrounding the homes," he remarked as the bus drove along the desert highway connecting the ancient cities of Alexandria and Cairo. "They house pigeons, which is a delicacy here."

Traveling on the bus back to the ship they discussed the culture, religion and politics of the area while other passengers fell into deep sleep. She heard murmurs from the passengers about how happy they were to be back on the air-conditioned vehicle and out of the dust and heat of the desert; she heard a few people discussing the amazing traffic congestion in the city, or the necessity for the security guard seated in the front of the bus in case of trouble on the highway on the way back to Alexandria where the ship was docked for the night; she heard one man in the seat behind them remark to his wife "I don't know what the big deal is, just a pile of rocks you have seen in a thousand pictures;" and she felt herself oh so grateful that she was seated next to a person who found something to delight in at every site they visited despite the number of times he had been to them.

She slowly found out a bit about Mark's personal life over quiet dinners at sea. He, unlike Roger, had not grown up in a privileged environment and his family had struggled to put him through college with the help of student loans and scholarship money. They had hoped he would become an estate lawyer or judge or CEO of a fortune 500 company. Instead he had ambled through college not knowing what he truly wanted in the future and getting a generic "Business degree." After graduating he joined an advertising firm in New York and started paying back all the loans he had accumulated. He had been somewhat disillusioned with the steady grind of work day after day though the loan amounts were diminishing quickly. After a few years of living in North Jersey and commuting into the city, working in a really unfulfilling job, and the ending of two unsatisfactory relationships, he was restless and depressed, not knowing really what he wanted to do but knew he wanted to see more of the world. That is when he met Andrew who by then was working in London.

They met at a party thrown by a mutual acquaintance at one of the firms whose business they were both courting.

"I would love to tell you I chose to do something truly altruistic such as joining the Peace Corp, but in truth Andrew re-sparked my interest in travel and a few months later I found myself following him to London to work with him."

"I really enjoyed London, found the city fascinating and Andrew and I would travel as much as possible to see the other 'close by' famous cities such as Paris and Barcelona whenever we had time. Long story short, I soon found myself once again disillusioned with the sales/advertising business and to be honest I was just no good with it. Andrew on the other hand is a genius in his field and was quickly becoming a rising international player in the advertising industry. I was good with people, still wanted to travel, was coming out of a failed romance with a British woman I had met, and Andrew came to my rescue once more. The cruise line was a client of ours and they were looking for an assistant cruise director, and the rest is history. I signed on this Italian cruise line and have worked my way up to having 'my own ship, the Columbus'. It is a good fit for this stage of my life."

"I have been doing this for almost ten years now and not only do I get to see briefly the ports that the ship travels to, but then on my six week leave every three months I get to travel back to the places that most interested me and the cultures I want to learn more about."

She could tell how truthful and content he was with his life when he continued, "I know this job would probably seem a bit frivolous and unimportant to many, certainly not altruistic and unfailingly helpful to people, but I do feel I provide in some small way to the joy in people's lives and feel that it is important for people to take time to relax, enjoy life, and that then they are more productive and happy in whatever avenue of life they are involved in when they return to work."

"What about your personal life," Carolyn found herself asking, "Don't you want more in that area?"

"No, I guess that is why Andrew and I became such good friends over the years as we are much alike in that respect. We both are quite selfish in what we want out of life. Sure I have had relationships with women over the years, and even have ended up with some great friendships out of some of those relationships, but marriage and family are just not for everybody."

She could see that he regretted the words as soon as they left his lips, and that he was quite embarrassed being as he was talking to a woman who was halfway through her first pregnancy and alone.

She felt he had given her the opening to ask the question she had been wondering about.

"So what exactly has Andrew told you about my situation?"

He looked directly into her eyes when he said "Not nearly enough."

He continued, "I would do anything for a friend, and Andrew certainly qualifies in that area. However over these last few weeks I find myself wanting to know you better. What he did tell me was that you knew each other in college, had been 'more than good friends' and that the relationship ended when he graduated and moved to London. He said he had kept track of your life off and on over the years as he never really had gotten you out of his system. He said you reconnected recently and then that you had called and said you had a 'situation' and needed help. He said he was happy to be back in touch with you and more than happy to help."

He took a sip of his drink before continuing, "I also was happy to help, and don't want to pry, but would really love to know you better and be helpful in any way I can also."

And so Carolyn found herself expanding a bit on her past telling him again the mostly true version of her life i.e. regarding her marriage to Roger (minus the location in Virginia), pregnancy after a short affair as she had mentioned to him earlier. But she also told him of Andrew's help in her "disappearance from her previous life... what she did not tell him was that Andrew had created a false identity for her nor that he was the father of her child. She would continue to be Sarah Church as far as Mark Donaldson was concerned.

She continued on sea days to research and read about the ports they would visit and Mark was a great help in filling in fun "not so well known" places, facts about each location that she could include in her articles. She spent her days at sea quietly observing and listening to the conversations of the passengers for clues of what they liked and disliked about sea travel, both the seasoned and unseasoned traveler.

At night she relaxed by reading philosophy and astronomy books as she watched the constellations above. On a floating hotel with upwards of 2000 people on board she found her quiet solace on her balcony on dark nights with the stars as her only companions, feeling like a tiny being in this vast universe floating out in the middle of nowhere. She was quite content.

She had just a few months to come to her senses and make her fateful decision. The more her child had grown within her the more she loved the little being she was about to give birth to and also the more she knew she had to make the choice she was so dreading. She wanted more than anything to spend every moment of every future day with her child, no matter where they would live or how she would manage to support the two of them, and at the same time she knew also that this traveling/writing vagabond type life would probably be the worst thing for the child who she realized needed a more stable upbringing. Her money would be running out. She could not seek a nursing job as "Sarah Church" had no nursing license. Her only means of supporting herself and the child was to keep on writing and traveling which would mean finding somewhere for her daughter/son to have a more normal childhood. She could not stand the thought of putting the child in a foster home, or into a stranger's home while she pursued her travel writing, which of course involved traveling (duh!).

As the ensuing months passed she thought several times of confronting Andrew and letting him be part of that decision, thus not having the choice left entirely up to her, but then on one of her brief on-shore breaks between sailings met Helen, his new partner. Turns out after years of frolicking, Andrew had seemingly found a true soul mate, a person whom he had known for years but recently was trying out a more intimate relationship. As he put it "someone he could really talk to about his innermost feelings, desires and fears, someone who enjoyed a carefree life with no thoughts of settling in any one place, just travelling and intellectually pursuing their individual dreams, someone who didn't judge him by society's rules." He said they had started out as friends, found they loved the same cities, the same art, food, museums, books, and they both had a fervent fondness of traveling to explore new cultures. He had grown tired of the relationship games he was playing with various women, knowing that the majority of them were much more serious about a future together than he was ever going to be and thus knowing each relationship would end badly. The sex had even gotten routine and as he had gotten older not quite as exciting as it once had been. As he said to Carolyn, "anyone who tells you they have a wonderful sex life in middle age forgets what a wonderful sex life is, or had never really experienced it in their younger years." However he had discovered with Helen an intimacy and trust and a shared zest for life about what was around the next corner. She was British, independently wealthy and therefore their pursuit of travel was not a problem. Andrew was once more investigating all of life's choices and as he rambled on about Helen, Carolyn couldn't help thinking that that was the type of life he had once talked about sharing with her. To add to her misery, in describing to Carolyn his relationship with Helen he even said to her: "You are the only other person I have ever felt I could be completely open with, no pretenses, no saying what one is expected to say in any given situation, just purely being me and not being judged for who I am." He and Helen had moved in together in her apartment in London although they were rarely there at the same time due to their business and social schedules. As he forthrightly put it, "I am not sure how this will play out, but for now we are enjoying one another's companionship. Right now I am realizing for the first time perhaps that true intimacy is just as meaningful as sex. Guess the experts might be right after all that a man reaches his sexual peak in his 20's, the rest is all about the relationship."

No, she once again thought to herself, he definitely was not ready for the news that he was about to have a child as he investigated this new chapter of his life. He had continued to be there whenever she needed something and assured her he would always be there for her in the future. She had no intentions of ever going back to Charlottesville, that chapter of her life was definitely over, and it looked like Andrew was about to disappear into his next adventure. She had to face the fact that she was now completely alone in deciding wherein her future and that of her child would lie.

Terri had informed her via her letters that Jenny was slowly and carefully inserting herself into Roger's life the past few months without being too pushy about it, just being sure Roger continued being active at the club and included in the ongoing social life there. She had convinced him he needed to be socially active in the community as it was good for both him and his medical practice as well. Carolyn suspected that relationship would continue to grow and in a strange way she was happy for him. He had found what he was looking for in Jenny and it seemed as though Jenny had gotten what she had wanted since they were an item in college. They deserved each other and their blissful money-filled superficial social life. She had no regrets on that front. She did wonder if Jenny would be so ready to commit to marriage though and knew Roger would want to make their situation legal so as to conform to society rules and thus be better for his professional reputation and career. She followed their ongoing saga via Terri's letters as if it was just a soap opera on television, already feeling no real emotional connection to her past life.

She in turn poured out her changing feelings to Terri via her letters. She vacillated between giving up the writing and finding a more stable land-based career and raising her child (probably in poverty) or perhaps finding a temporary foster home for the child while she established herself in her writing career so she could then reclaim her child. Neither option really sounded good, and time was moving forward. Terri insisted when she reached her ninth month that she stay put in Barcelona, and that she and hopefully Jeff would come spend the month with her. After all, they didn't want her going through this momentous occasion alone, and certainly didn't want the child born on a cruise ship somewhere in the Mediterranean, or worse yet in one of the ports they were visiting. Carolyn was grateful for the offer and looked forward to seeing them.

The articles she had submitted after her first cruise on Alexandria and Cairo were accepted by a travel magazine, and the Italian cruise line loved her little tour write ups for the ship's brochure. She would have time for a couple of more short 14-21 day cruises before her delivery date. Fortunately the Columbus was staying in the Mediterranean until spring. However, the writing certainly was not bringing in much money and she was quickly using up the money she had taken from her joint account with Roger.

Most satisfyingly of all she had started a real friendship with Sasha during those first few cruises and her final decision regarding the precious life within her came out of her many long talks with Sasha. She had needed a female confidant as she continued her voyages on the Columbus and although Sasha was much younger than Carolyn they grew increasingly fond of each other. Sasha talked at length of her life and its strange twists and turns. She had been born to a single mother in Russia. Her mother had no way of supporting her and she was put into a Russian orphanage. She remembered really nothing about those first couple of years nor did she remember her mother. At 4 years of age she was adopted by an American couple and her life had seemed a fairy tale to her since then. Carolyn and Sasha spent many days together while the majority of passengers were off on shore excursions, talking together, discussing philosophy books they were both reading, and talking of life's strange twists.

"How did you feel about being adopted?" Carolyn finally had the courage to ask the all-important question that she had really wanted to ask since learning that Sasha was adopted, "How do you feel about your birth mother having given you up?"

She and Sasha were sitting on one of the main decks under a beautiful star filled sky at her favorite time of day, when the night time shows were over, the casinos closed, and only the cleaning crew and a few stragglers were left wandering the ship.

Sasha was quiet for a moment. "You know, you would think a person would be curious about that, especially with the trends now of looking up your family tree and tracing your ancestors, and of course of knowing your medical history. But the truth is, I have very few memories of the orphanage itself either good or bad, and really no memory of my biological mother, perhaps those are memories that might come out in self-analysis/psychotherapy someday if I ever chose to go that route, which believe me I don't."

She got more serious as she continued to talk. "My earliest memories really are just of a typical childhood in a small town by the ocean in New Jersey, with a loving mom and dad who provided me a steady wonderful childhood along with a good education."

"When did you discover they were not your biological parents? How did that make you feel toward your biological parents for leaving you with someone else?"

Carolyn held her breath waiting for the answer.

"I know this probably will sound strange to you, but my adoptive parents were always very honest from the beginning. I don't remember any definitive solemn moment where they sat me down to tell me that I was adopted, but somehow they always let me know that I was from Russia, that they had brought me to America when I was a child so that they could give me a good life and that they loved me very much. Like any child growing up what really mattered to me were my friends, my warm and loving home, and the sense of security and love that I was surrounded with in that home."

"How did you feel about your birth mother, did you resent her, were you curious about what she was like or why she gave you up, did you or do you ever want to find her?" These obviously were the questions that were on Carolyn's mind, and she had always been afraid to ask them for fear of what the answers would be.

Sasha looked directly into Carolyn's eyes as she said, "To be truthful, I never really think about my biological parents, although I realize that that may not be what you want to hear. I guess they are just not real to me."

Sasha saw through Carolyn's reasons for asking all these questions and knew she was struggling with the upcoming decision she had to make. As mentioned, they had had many long talks over the past few cruises. However she did not want to lie to her or sugar-coat the idea of the reality that she was truly neutral in her feelings about her biological parents, she neither resented them nor did she have any desire to know anything more about them. She went on to say that she figured her biological mother had a reason for choosing the path she did, and who was she to judge her? She had been brought up with the two people she truly considered her mom and dad. Having studied to be a nurse if there was anything she might be curious about it would only be her medical history.

Carolyn appreciated her honesty. She was realizing more and more as her due date approached what she had to do to ensure her child had a happy, caring and safe upbringing, she also knew that she would regret this decision for the rest of her life. It was the price she was willing to pay. She could not be selfish about this important decision. She wrote a letter to Terri and Jeff that evening:

My dearest friends:
As the date for my child's delivery approaches I am struggling every moment with a decision I know I must face………………….

She went on to expand on her reasons for wanting her child to have a stable home life with a loving mother and father, and her knowledge that Terri and Jeff had longed for a child of their own which had just never happened. She concluded the letter by saying:

I know this is a momentous decision for you, and you know though it is surely a heartbreaking one for me, I feel certain it is the correct decision my future child. Please think this through, call me and/or if you think it possible, come and discuss the options with me.

My love to you both, C.

She was offering her child to her best friends, and she knew she would always regret it.

MAY 1980
KARA'S BIRTH

As the time drew near for her delivery she and Terri had some of the most important and hardest conversations of her life. She spent many sleepless nights alone in her Barcelona apartment during her ninth month as she was no longer safe to travel. She talked constantly to the little person inside her and wept as she did so. Someday she hoped this precious child would understand how hard this was for her but how sure she was that the child would have a better life in a loving two parent stable middle class household than with a single, traveling, working mother who would have to constantly leave him/her in someone else's care while she made the money to support the two of them, be it with her writing or a simple "day job." Terri and Jeff had been thrilled as they read of Carolyn's plan and agreed immediately. They had wanted a child desperately and when despite fertility treatments a successful pregnancy had not occurred they had talked often of adoption. The right time had just never presented itself. They set off as quickly as arrangements could be made to join Carolyn in Barcelona for the birth. They needed to be sure that all three of them agreed this was not a temporary deal, it was an irreversible decision for all of them.

Those last few weeks before the delivery, Terri and Jeff came and stayed with Carolyn in Barcelona. Terri and Carolyn walked the beach each morning discussing the upcoming event which would change all of their lives forever. Terri kept assuring her that should she change her mind, even after seeing the baby, that she and Jeff would understand completely, they did not want to force her into anything and would stand by her in her choice. She and Jeff being the only people who knew that Andrew was the father of this child did present a concern.

"Jeff and I keep thinking of Andrew's situation," Terri confided one morning. "Perhaps he should be part of this discussion?"

"Absolutely not" was Carolyn's vehement response. "I have thought about this for nearly nine months. It is not news that he would welcome, it would change his life and not for the better. He is a good person, but I do not want him 'sacrificing' his life nor my child's life trying to 'do the right thing' and thus making them both miserable in the long run. Believe me I have put a lot of thought into this and it is the right decision!"

She continued, "The only thing that is enabling me to keep my sanity through this most difficult time is the fact that I know my child will grow up in a happy, stable, two-parent household with people who want and love her/him completely and who have chosen to make raising her/him the most important thing in their lives."

The three of them did not speak of Andrew's part in the upcoming birth again.

"I do have to tell you however," Terri began as they continued their beach walk one morning, "if you decide this arrangement is best for the child's future and for all involved, and we sign the adoption papers, that decision will then have to be permanent."

Carolyn could see the sadness and sincerity in Terri's eyes.

"Jeff and I have longed for a child since we got married and as you know unfortunately that didn't happen. I can assure you we would love, cherish and provide for this child and strive to be the best parents possible."

Her voice cracked and the seriousness of her tone came through as she continued, "However, once the baby goes home with us I would never be able to part with him/her. We would be the child's parents from that point forward."

Carolyn's hand reflexively rested on her belly feeling the child's movements as she fought back her tears. She knew that no matter how hard this was going to be for her, that she was making the right choice for the child.

Jeff joined them at what had become their favorite little coffee shop at the end of the beach and the conversation took on a lighter tone.

Kara was born a few weeks later, and thanks to a very modern and understanding nurse-midwife, and the fact that Terri was a nurse and Jeff a doctor, at Carolyn's request all three were in the birthing room.

If Carolyn had thought the previous months making this decision were hard, it was nothing compared to the few days after Kara's birth. Jeff had tried to tell her how emotional it would be for her to see the child and then give her up, but she insisted that she needed to hold the baby, feel her, feed her, and spend some time with her absorbing every little detail. She wanted to remember everything about the child. She knew Terri would send pictures and updates, but she did not know when or if she would ever see Kara again. She reveled in being with her and cried her eyes out each of the next three nights. How could she ever be sure this was the right thing to do? This was the moment she had dreamed of forever, holding her own baby in her arms, loving her, and caring for her for the rest of her life. She traced her eyebrows with her finger, her lips, her toes, her fingers. She felt she could not bear the pain she knew would follow when Kara left and became part of a new family. She felt she was spiraling toward madness each time they returned her child to the nursery.

When Andrew came to see her she almost lost it. She had been hoping he and Helen would be away somewhere on their travels so she wouldn't have to deal with and see him at this time, hoped he would send a heartfelt apology for not being with her. No such luck.

"Are you kidding me," Andrew said with such levity. "How could I not be here for you at this moment?"

She knew he was sincere feeling he was providing moral support in what he knew was the most difficult decision she had faced in her life. When she learned Andrew was coming to see her she had made Terri swear not to leave her alone with him. She had to keep things light and the conversation superficial. She was almost sure he would guess the baby's heritage when he saw Kara's beautiful eyes and coloring that already were looking like her father. Terri too struggled with her conscience, as much as she really really wanted to raise Kara, and already loved her dearly, wasn't it totally unfair to Andrew to not let him be part of this decision? Ironically it was Terri who also felt she could not be alone with Andrew.

As it turned out, it was Helen who never left them alone. As she and Andrew tried to cheer Carolyn with the tales of their upcoming adventures, Carolyn slipped into an even darker depression. She felt her life was over, but at least Kara's was just beginning.

Sasha also visited while the Columbus was in port. She was not totally surprised and was supportive of Carolyn's decision and kept reassuring her that Kara would be just fine. She tried to keep things as light as possible, but she was truly concerned about Carolyn's state of mind and promised she would visit on her next shipboard leave. Even Sasha's visit couldn't cheer her.

"How did you ever find such a perfect couple to raise your Kara?" Sasha was gushing on and on about how wonderful Jeff and Terri were, as she and Carolyn took a walk out on the hospital lawn one afternoon. Unlike everyone else who were trying to have Carolyn look ahead and not back, Sasha did not shy from talking about Kara. She knew the child was all that was on

Carolyn's mind and saw no use pretending otherwise. Carolyn slipped easily back into her "Sarah Church" mode.

"Actually Andrew had met them in the states a few years ago, and remembered them. He told me about the small town in Virginia where they lived, how they had longed for a child, and as Andrew does he just took over, got me in contact with them and the rest is history." She was not about to tell Sasha her true life story, the less people knew of her background the better she would be able to maintain her identity as Sarah Church. She had to trust that Andrew felt that way also and would have to make sure he went along with this latest addition to her "cover story."

"Well they both certainly gained my trust just over this short period I have spent with them. They are so sincere, so obviously thrilled to have Kara, and you can just tell she will have the best life that they can provide for her." Carolyn felt herself sinking into a deeper and deeper depression as Sasha gushed on and on about how perfect everything was turning out.

A few days later baby Kara went home to America to become Kara Mullins and be raised in Charlottesville, Virginia as the well cared for and well-loved daughter of a small town physician and his lovely wife. Their friends at the country club thought it wonderful that they were so fortunate to have found an American child through an International Adoption Agency and they all just assumed the biological mother was simply a single American ex-pat living abroad, probably some avant-guard artsy type. They all politely did not question the happy new parents. That was the social code after all.

Terri and Jeff had agreed to let Kara know when she was old enough to understand that although she was adopted they loved her as their own and felt very blessed to have her in their lives. With both of them being in the medical profession Terri and Jeff both felt Kara should know her true family medical history and wanted to be honest about her origins. Carolyn would discreetly probe into Andrew's medical history when the timing was right. It would then be up to Kara as she grew older to decide how much if any information she wanted regarding her biological parents. Terri promised to keep Carolyn informed of Kara's growing-up years, and Carolyn agreed in turn never to contact Kara unless she expressed a wish to meet her biological mother when she got older.

ONE YEAR LATER
JUNE 1981

Carolyn meanwhile had sunk further and further into her deeply depressive state.

Still unsuspecting, Andrew had flown over a few times for short visits hoping to help her out of her post-partum depression. She had taken a year off from the cruise line job knowing that although physically she could possibly resume her job, she also knew she would be in no shape mentally to go back to work after the traditional six weeks maternity leave. She was going to need more time than that to digest the twists of fate that had led her to what should have been her happiest moment in life, and now was quite bittersweet. She had felt confident that sacrificing her future with her daughter was the price she must pay for her daughter having a happy and successful life with two loving parents, but no matter how much she told herself this, it did not help. Each time she saw young mothers strolling down the beach with their children she became more withdrawn and began to isolate herself in her apartment. She eventually told Andrew that she appreciated his concern, but that she just needed some time alone and that she would contact him when she was ready to confront life again. What she didn't say was that she just could not face him right now as each time she saw him she faced the fantasy that perhaps she should tell him the truth, that with his connections he would help her get Kara back from her adoptive parents, and that the three of them would live happily ever after. After a few weeks of her refusing every offer to get her out of her apartment, Andrew had seen that there was nothing he could do at the moment, and left to attend to his business affairs, but with the firm commitment that he was not going to allow her to wallow in self-pity very long. He had put her in touch with a psychiatrist and made her promise to take the medicine the doctor was prescribing for her, to get some fresh air, eat well, and he would be back shortly. She was unable to do any writing as she could not concentrate on anything for very long.

Her life-line and what kept her sanity was the weekly letter from Terri and Jeff documenting Kara's progress and always accompanied by a photo. She re-read the letters over and over each evening, at times beginning with the first letter she had received when they brought Kara home 13 months ago, sometimes just picked a random letter out of the box to read, sometimes keeping the latest letter by her bedside table along with the most recent photo to stare at when she could not sleep. She explained to the psychiatrist that she needed to do this to assure herself that she had not lost her mind, and that Kara was real:

June 1980…
My dearest friend:

Jeff and I will always be in your debt. The trip back to Charlottesville went smoothly, Kara is going to be a great traveler as she is learning at an early age. Although we wondered if we could pull off the "adoption thing" in the community without anyone associating the baby with our friendship with you and your sudden disappearance, that doesn't seem to be a connection being made in anyone else's eyes. I surely thought Jenny would be suspicious, but if she is she has not uttered a word. Everyone has their public-face on, is congratulating us "sincerely" and ooh-ing and ahh-ing over Kara (as well they should be as she is the most beautiful and well behaved baby ever....ha ha)....

September 1980
...Jenny continues to help Roger get back into the social scene at the club, and he keeps busy with his sports and his medical practice. Jeff sees less and less of him outside those areas, and that is the way we plan to keep it. We are now slowly beginning to form a new social group consisting of "new parent" friends.

I have gone back to work in Jeff's office, and we just carry Kara along to work daily with us. I promise you she will never lack for anything, least of all love.

Jeff and I think of you 24 hours a day and hope you will carry on in your life and find some peace and perhaps even joy knowing that with your personal sacrifice you have provided your daughter a safe and loving home. Please take care of yourself and keep in touch with us. I will continue to keep you updated as to

Kara's progress, with pics of course.   Please keep us
updated as to your well being as well.

With love and gratitude, Terri

The subsequent letters and pictures were full of cheer and reassurance that Kara was doing just fine and Terri and Jeff continued to encourage her to please keep them apprised of what was happening in her life. Short notes of gratitude for the updates and pictures were all that Carolyn had been able to manage to this point.

JANUARY 1982

Six months later, inspired by Terri's letters, and Sasha's and Mark's phone calls and visits when the Columbus was in Barcelona, and of course she was sure from the effects of the antidepressant medication and counseling she was receiving, Carolyn awoke one morning and decided it was time she stopped with the self-pity and begin making something of the rest of her life. She had done what she considered best for Kara, and there was no way to change that now. She had her days and nights of doubt but overall still felt Kara was better off with Terri and Jeff in a stable home than she would have been with her alone. She was paying dearly for her decision and had slipped into a morbid stagnant state accompanied by a bit too much wine at night. She knew this needed to stop. Terri and Jeff were to raise Kara as their own child and had agreed to let her know when she was old enough to understand that although she was adopted they loved her as their own and felt so blessed to have her in their lives. It would be up to Kara as she grew older to decide how much information she wanted about her biological parents. What more could Carolyn ask for than that, at least it provided some hope for once again seeing her sometime in the future. She thought of Kara every day, but knew from Terri's letters and the pictures she enclosed that she was happy and well taken care of and Carolyn was certain she had done the right thing although the pain of that decision would always be with her. She devoured books about adoptive children and the psychological impact on them. Seeing Sasha so carefree and well-adjusted reassured her each time they got together. It was way too soon to contemplate what Kara's decision would be when she was older since after all Kara at this point was still barely a toddler.

These thoughts of the possibility that someday she still might have contact with Kara and a chance to explain her motives and actions finally broke through Carolyn's depressive haze. She decided that along with writing to Terri and Jeff, she would also enclose separate letters to Kara so that when the timing was right, and if and when Kara ever began asking questions about her biological parents, Terri could give her the letters and Kara would know that her biological mother had never stopped thinking of her or loving her. She would enclose a sealed letter to her daughter with each future letter to Terri. This thought gave her the motivation to move on with her life, begin making some money for Kara's future inheritance, and let her know her mother never forgot her for even a second.

She would keep her promise to Terri and Jeff not to initiate that contact herself. She began enclosing the letters to Kara in her letters to Terri, to be opened only in the event that if later in life Kara expressed the desire to know about her biological mother so they would be a source of information for her of Carolyn's reason for her decision and of the love that she had always felt for Kara. This acted as a cathartic and a motive for Carolyn to lead a better life herself. She, Terri and Jeff would all leave the decision of what to do about the letters up to Kara as she grew into womanhood many years from now.

SARAH MOVES ON
SUMMER 1982

She continued taking her daily walks down to the beach, having coffee and a light breakfast and watching the cruise ships come and go from the nearby dock. She started to read about the Catalonian history and culture and explore the Gaudy architecture of Barcelona. She began to write once again with a renewed fervor and even a bit of excitement for the first time in quite a while. She tried 'people-watching', observing little details, listening to bits of strangers' conversations on the beach in the early a.m. and at sunset, as she had once again begun the process of mastering the language. She now turned to books about writing novels, absorbing details, paying attention to small details of her surroundings. She read everything she could find on the process of publishing a novel. She cut down on the wine so her mind would be sharper. She decided she could not change any decisions of the past and thus started in on the next chapter of her life. She began to collect data for her first mystery novel, set amongst the background of the city of Barcelona. Her main character would be a nurse on a cruise ship whose main port of departure at the moment was this lovely port on the northeastern coast of Spain.

PREPARATIONS
SUMMER 1982

As her 40th birthday came closer, Carolyn decided she needed to get out amongst people more so as not to drift back into a deep depression as that important milestone loomed in her mind. She had made a lot of mistakes these first forty years and she was going to remedy that in the next forty.

She was still writing frequent letters not only to Terri and Jeff, but also to the daughter she hoped to one day meet, just how that would happen she had no idea but the thread of certainty that it would happen kept her going, and she knew she had to get on with her life in the meantime. Terri and Jeff continued to send updates and pictures of Kara. The smiling child in the pictures and the stories of her growth and development did little to ease the pain in Carolyn's heart, but did convince her that her daughter was thriving in a very loving family. Carolyn knew she now had to continue on with her life, and she would do so by pursuing the only avenue she could see open to her.

First problem to tackle was that she was just about totally out of money. She had managed to complete her first mystery novel with the heroine being a cruise ship nurse, but had no idea how to go about possibly getting it published. Sasha and Mark had been great resources for her novel and she picked their brain about different cruise-life scenarios that she came up with to make sure they were plausible. Now she needed a more immediate source of income to begin the next chapter of her life.

With Mark's help she contacted the Italian cruise line on which she had previously sailed and written for and they were happy to have her once again come on board, at her own expense of course as a freelance writer, submit her travel writings for publication in travel magazines as previously and also in the cruise line brochures if corporate office thought they were deemed as worthwhile as her earlier submissions had been. The Columbus was in dry dock at present being refurbished and once more updated, however the Italian line also owned a ship called The Isabella that was leaving Honolulu on a 14 day round trip of the Hawaiian islands in late October if she wanted to sail on that. She had approximately four months to find a publisher and get herself to Honolulu! What better way to get future material for the next mystery novel in the series than to get back on a new ship. She accepted the offer, and began to plot how to get there.

She once again asked Andrew for help, thinking what the hell he owed her some help didn't he, even though he had no idea why. He agreed to subsidize the expenses of the trip to Hawaii for her until she could get her bearings once again. She promised that this time it was merely a loan until she could become financially independent. He once again deposited a hefty amount of cash into the original account he had set up for "Sarah

Church" nearly three years ago when she had first arrived in Barcelona.

He also, full of surprises as always, steered her in the direction of a literary agent who just might be interested in reading the first draft of her mystery novel. She once again overlooked how he did things, was just grateful that he did. He was actually ecstatic to see her coming out of her self-imposed isolation of the past year. She happily took both the money, and the name of the agent, and set about submitting her query letter, synopsis, and the first draft of what was to become a well-known mystery series. She even asked Sasha's permission to further pick her brain for ideas. Her main character's name, the heroine of the series would of course be named Kara.

FALL 1982
KEY WEST, FLORIDA

She had never been to Hawaii, knew nothing about the islands the Isabella would be visiting, and so had a lot of prep work to do, but knew she had to pursue her writing in order to having a purpose in life before she went mad. This was to be her legacy for Kara. Andrew took it upon himself to propose a short vacation together before restarting her career. They were sharing a pitcher of Sangria at what had become her favorite tapas restaurant when he mentioned he and Helen were flying to Miami in a couple of weeks and why didn't she join them.

"Have you ever been to the Florida Keys?"

She looked at him in complete shock. "Look, I am totally grateful with all you are doing to help me once again 'start over', but I have just about a month to prepare for this upcoming Hawaiian voyage, not to mention tie up my life here in Barcelona and submit my mystery manuscript to Sergio. I hardly think I can just up and go to the Keys with you and Helen."

He went on to explain that all his agent-friend Sergio needed at the moment was the rough first draft she had sent to see what potential the novel had, that he and Helen were finding that they made good traveling companions and friends, but nothing more.

Since we all are planning to travel west to the states, I think it only fitting that we all give ourselves a two week 'vacation' before you start off on your upcoming venture in the Hawaiian islands, I do go north to do some business, and Helen goes off to visit some friends in the Northeast."

He looked at her sincerely, "I am not going to let you disappear from my life again, it is just so good to see you returning to your former self again. No serious plans, just friends relaxing together for a couple of weeks. I promise I will have you in Hawaii in plenty of time for the Isabella's sailing. I am happy to make all the arrangements if you would allow me to."

"It does sound wonderful to have traveling companions at least on the first leg of the trip, and no I have never seen the Florida Keyes," she heard herself saying as she thought to herself once again: Can I really trust myself to spend a leisurely couple of weeks alone with them without revealing the truth about Kara?

Andrew continued, "It will be fun, we will bike, eat seafood, drink wine, and just relax."

He was as convincing as ever and while sipping on the sangria and looking out at the sunset, she found herself saying "why not?"

A few weeks later the three of themselves found themselves in the Miami airport after an uneventful flight.

"When you have lived and worked most of your life in major cities, believe me a vacation where you can live in shorts and sandals, no make-up, and just completely relax in sunshine sounds like heaven to me."

Helen was really looking forward to just "kicking back" and Carolyn was finding it hard not to like her. They waited together while Andrew picked up the rental car. They had left the trip-planning entirely up to him and were more than ready to take no responsibility over the next two weeks and just follow his lead. This was his business and he excelled at it.

He pulled up shortly in a luxury convertible and loaded in the luggage. Seasoned travelers as they were Andrew and Helen had really packed quite compactly, and Carolyn following their lead was having the cruise line take care of getting most of her luggage to the ship in Hawaii. So here they were 3 middle age adults feeling and acting and as if they were back in college and on spring break.

"So, where are we off to kind sir?" Helen said as she slipped into the front seat and Carolyn dutifully took her place in the back seat, however even this position as 'third wheel' on the trip was not going to dampen her determination to totally relax these two weeks. She simply decided to relish this chance before the adventures of Sarah Church's life began once again.

Andrew proceeded to tell them how a friend of his had a little house on the water in Key Largo, the first of the Keyes, which he had kindly made available to them while he was away. A short time later they pulled into the driveway of this amazing residence. It was on a canal leading to the ocean with views across the harbor to the ocean. Carolyn was given her choice of the guest bedroom suite on the main floor or the guest apartment on the lower level complete with hot tub and swimming pool on its patio, and its own private entrance. She chose the latter. After getting the luggage to the proper rooms and taking a quick shower, they went for short ride along the beach road, had a few drinks and a lovely informal seafood dinner and went back to the house for the night. Carolyn felt like a queen in her own luxurious guest quarters and vowed to sleep forever beneath the sumptuous covers. She was amazed that she had absolutely zero feelings about what Andrew and Helen were up to in the main residence master bedroom just above her.

She awoke to a knock on the door the next morning.

"Carolyn, are you awake yet?" When she opened the door Andrew was standing there with tray in hand containing coffee, pastry, fresh fruit and even a fresh flower on the tray.

"It is much too beautiful to sleep the day away." He said as he opened the door to the patio and led her to a table by the small pool.

She grabbed her robe and sleepily followed him. "Where is Helen?" she inquired still quite sleepily.

"She went off for a run. I am afraid she has quite a bit more energy than I in the mornings" he said laughingly.

"I thought this might be a good time to talk privately, as we may not get too many opportunities like this" he continued as he pulled out her chair.

"Well, for one thing you must remember to call me Sarah, or does Helen know 'the whole story'?" She said as she sat down. The coffee smelled wonderful. He

127

was still quite a thoughtful man and it was during times like this that she still felt the urge to open up to him about Kara.

"So, are you really doing as well on the inside as you appear to be on the outside?" He went on while pouring the coffee. It seems his friend had also left the house stocked with basic necessities food wise for them, meaning coffee, breakfast muffins, fruit and wine.

"I made the hardest decision I hope I will ever have to make," Carolyn said honestly. "Now I must move on, we shall see if I am able to do that." He still was easy to talk to, and so hard not to have the conversation with him that it was so tempting to have.

"Terri and Jeff are keeping me updated on Kara's progress, and that is comforting." She was on the verge of continuing by asking if he wanted to see a picture of her, but was not sure she could handle watching him stare at the picture of his own daughter.

"So, tell me how things are going with Helen." She quickly changed the subject before things got too deep. This was going to be her two weeks to totally relax and she was going to keep it light. Too late for changes of heart now.

Andrew went on to tell her of how Helen and he had a great relationship, fun traveling together, yet both independently living their own lives also. "The best of both worlds" as he put it, and he emphasized that both of them were happy with it that way. "This way when we go off separately we always have things to talk about when we get back together. None of the dull conversations married people must have when they start doing everything together." He smiled as he made the meant-to-be funny remark but she could tell he was absolutely being truthful underneath the surface humor.

Ah yes, Carolyn thought, Helen was the independent-minded woman she could never have been, reaffirming her life was unfolding as it should be.

"As a matter of fact after our two week hiatus here I am headed for D.C. and Helen for New York. She has a friend there who is going to show her the sights."

Carolyn didn't even ask if it were a male friend or female friend she was meeting, she was ready to get off this subject. She also was too afraid to broach the subject of he and Jenny, was he planning a visit to Charlottesville while doing business in D.C. she wondered.....

A short silence ensued.

"So tell me about these mystery novels you are writing," Andrew was ready to keep it light and impersonal also. She had told no one but Sasha and Mark the themes for what she hoped would become a popular series. She was waiting anxiously to hear what Andrew's agent-friend Sergio would think of the manuscript.

"Well, my heroine will be a single woman working as a nurse on a cruise ship and thus her work involves travel all over the world, making the perfect setting for stumbling into adventure, romance and intrigue and mystery." She found herself actually wanting to tell him about her stories, and he seemed genuinely interested.

"Well, I do have an extensive travel background, so If I can help with any details of the places your heroine will be visiting let me know," he found himself saying. "You know the old adage 'write about what you know'."

Her face lit up. "That might actually help me add some 'filler stuff' to the books, while I concentrate on the characters, plots etc. Promise to send me lots and lot of info on day to day life in my chosen ports of call and I promise to thank you on the dedication page" she teased.

"Ah, so I can be helpful with 'filling in' space while you get to create the real story," he smiled as he poured her a second cup of coffee. "Sounds like you have already planned a whole series even as you have just submitted the first draft of the first book, Ms. Sarah Church, mystery novelist! I like that forward-thinking attitude! Reminds me of the girl I used to know in college those many years ago!"

Carolyn swore she saw a bit of admiration in his eyes for the energetic adventure-seeking young girl she once was back in their college years. She had to be careful not to encourage that route. They were obviously both just reminiscing in this relaxed atmosphere. The harmless bantering was fun though, and she was beginning to get a bit excited over her new project.

"Okay, I know we promised to keep these two weeks light, but while we are alone tell me how are you really doing after all that has taken place? I know the person you are too well to believe that you have really turned the corner into the future as yet, although I also know that you eventually will. I just want you to know you can call me anytime you need support, emotional, financial or otherwise." His eyes told her he truly meant it. Oh, if only she felt comfortable telling him how much he already was and always would be involved in her life story!

"Thank you" was all she could say. "You have been more than helpful these last two years and I truly owe you a big debt of gratitude. I hope to hear from your friend Sergio soon and see what he thinks and go from there!" Saying the agent's name out loud made her truly realize the reality of this big step and what it could mean for her future. "I don't know that I will ever get over letting Kara go, but life does go on and I do know she is happy. That is the best I can do right now, there is no turning back."

"Now, how about a quick dive into the pool before Helen comes back with a plan for the day?" She was determined to get back to their relaxing, 'no serious discussions,' two week hiatus.

And thus the two most relaxing weeks in the past year unfolded. The three of them actually cemented a renewed friendship as well as ate, swam and fished their way through several of the Keyes. Andrew even surprised her one evening by telling her he had rented clubs for them and gotten a tee time at his friend's club. Although she protested that she had not even picked up a club in 3 years, he refused to let her out of the plan simply stating, "just pitch and putt, pick up the ball whenever you like, and bring a camera. I can promise you will see more ibis here than anywhere else in the Keys...and when her blank look told him she had no idea of what he was talking about, he went on to tell her about the amazing local white birds she would be sure to spot on the course. Florida has some wonderful wildlife on their courses, birds, alligators etc., of course nothing like the scenery you will see on the Hawaiian courses." He was right as usual and although she wouldn't actually call what she did 'golf', she did enjoy the day immensely.

When the vacation drew to a close she felt somewhat revitalized and ready to start anew planning the legacy she could leave for Kara. She continued her letters to her as a means of saying all the things she wanted to say to her and might never have the opportunity. She always kept the latest picture of Kara with her.

They closed out the following week as all tourists in the Keys do, watching the sunset on the pier in Key West with drinks in hand. It had been a truly revitalizing couple of weeks and she found herself imagining a future once again for the first time in a couple of years.

The phone call from Sergio just added to her pleasure. He was submitting her manuscript for publication with a small publishing company in the States and would keep her posted. He told her not to get too excited as yet, but perhaps she would want to start on a second manuscript for the series so if the book did do well they would have an immediate sequel ready to go! He did not have to ask twice, she had already begun on her next shipboard adventure manuscript.

ONE FINAL MATTER

At the airport in Miami they headed off to three different terminals. Helen on her way to New York City to meet her friend, she would catch up in Dulles with Andrew in a few weeks and they would fly back to London together. Andrew off to D.C. for some business and a side trip to see Jenny in Charlottesville, and Carolyn off to Hawaii. Once again Carolyn wondered should she tell Andrew the truth about Kara, what if he ran into Terri and Jeff at the club with Kara, where she was sure Jenny would be showing Andrew off. How could he not see that she had his eyes! Worse yet, what if he ran into Roger, whatever Jenny knew, Roger was likely to know also as Jenny did love to spread news. Andrew assured Carolyn that as far as Jenny was concerned his contact with Carolyn had ended with her disappearance and he was as baffled as anyone as to what had happened. Terri and Jeff would "play their part" and acknowledge only that they had met Andrew the one weekend he had been at the club with Carolyn and Roger a couple of years prior. Ironically as Andrew's friendship with Jenny continued, it was another way that Carolyn would be able to hear news of Kara as the years went by, and Jenny's contacts were good for Andrew's business dealings. Practicing her new found serenity she decided she could not control who Andrew spoke to or encountered on his infrequent visits to Charlottesville, but she could control her own secrets and feelings. She could only hope that Andrew would be capable of 'playing his part' when with Jenny on his infrequent visits to Charlottesville and remember what he was 'supposed to know and not know.'

However before they all flew off in separate directions she had one more favor to ask of Andrew as she had another door to close on her past life before she could proceed onward, and he came through as always.

He found an international lawyer who contacted Roger on her behalf and got the divorce proceedings underway. The lawyer over time eventually somehow arranged to conceal where "Carolyn" was or what course her life had taken, only that she wanted a divorce and was willing for Roger to make the initial filing and thus control the settlement on the grounds that his wife had "abandoned him and the marriage." There was no mention made of Andrew. Andrew would continue to deny knowledge of her whereabouts. Carolyn received nothing out of the divorce settlement. She didn't really want anything from him and she was after all the one who left. He hopefully would never learn of the real reason she left so suddenly. As far as Roger, Jenny and the rest of the country club crowd they were all very happy for Terri and Jeff that things had worked for them in finding a child to adopt and that connection had never been questioned. Roger's friendship with Jeff was becoming a more a distant and professional relationship over the years as Roger and Jenny were both climbing the Country Club ladder as just friends, and Terri and Jeff were pursuing a quieter family life. With Andrew contacting the lawyer to get the divorce proceedings started, 'Sarah Church' was finally able and ready to move forward with her life.

HAWAII
OCTOBER 1982

Her first trip to the Hawaiian Islands became the next step on the ladder of building a life that would eventually benefit Kara at least financially, and hopefully with her becoming someone Kara could be proud to know some future day. Carolyn boarded the plane bound for Honolulu with a brighter attitude than she had had in the past two years. It was going to be a full very long day of travel. She was determined to make something of her life now that Kara's future was looking secure. She was even able to use the several flights and layovers that it took to go from Miami to Honolulu to delve into her research material she had collected on the culture of the islands she would be visiting, no longer the fearful flyer she once had been.

Unfortunately her flight from L.A. to Honolulu, the last leg of her long journey was delayed and she missed the ship's sailing, and of course her one piece of luggage had not accompanied her through all her many layovers. The airline promised to get the luggage to the ship when it arrived regardless of what port the ship was in when that happened. Apparently this was not an unusual occurrence. Certainly not an impressive start to her journey. She would have to remember in her article in the travel brochure to recommend never planning to arrive at your destination on the same day as your ship was departing, always to give yourself a day's extra time. On the plus side she had had most of her things shipped on ahead and so was just in need of some basics to get her through the next few hours until she could get to the ship where she assumed her belongings would be. She took a very expensive cab ride to a run-down hotel near the airport where the noise from the small bar next store kept her awake the remainder of the night. Certainly not what the travel brochures regarding Honolulu had promised! The next morning after a quick shower and essentially no sleep she contacted the cruise line and arranged a flight on Aloha Airlines to fly her to Hilo to meet the ship on their first stop there later that afternoon. She was exhausted but feeling quite good about independently taking charge of her life once again. She was quite a different person from the housewife of a couple of years ago. First stop breakfast, and then the shopping area to purchase some clothing to hold her over until the missing luggage arrived and she could hopefully meet up with her Barcelona belongings on the ship. Her total worldly possessions were very small at this point.

The flight from Honolulu to Hilo held about 20 people and flew low enough to see the layout of the islands. It was a sunny day and quite a magnificent view, more material for her brochure. She was getting excited. She took a cab from the airport to the seaport in Hilo where passengers were already disembarking for their first tours of the island and its famous volcano. She went quickly to the first tour bus and explained her position asking how long before the bus took off for the volcano, and if there was room for one more passenger. She was assured that if she got a ticket from the cruise director there was room for her. Next step, over to the security people on the ship's ramp where passengers were disembarking. Once again showing her credentials, ticket etc. she requested to speak to the cruise director.

"Welcome to the Isabella Ms. Church, we were sorry to hear of your travel delay."

She was looking into the face of a gentleman approximately her age, although very attractive and more sophisticated than she was sure she appeared to him. He introduced himself as Sam Allen, and she quickly explained her predicament to him.

"......and so you see, I cannot miss this opportunity to see the famous Kilauea volcano if I am to include it in the travel brochure."

He responded as if she had asked for something as simple as a drink of water or cup of coffee.

"Not a problem at all. I will have the desk print you up a tour ticket immediately. The tour returns at 6 p.m., at which time I will meet you at the travel desk in the lobby with your cabin keys. We can take care of all the boarding paper work at that time. We have taken the liberty of assigning you a cabin on Deck 7, with a balcony of course, so that you can write favorably about our beautiful ship." He said this with a conspiratorial smile.

"Now, let's let the security people take your picture so we can have your boarding badge ready for you when you return. We placed your pre-shipped belongings in your cabin, I assume the rest of your luggage is in the cab over there?"

With this she gave him a quick smile and handed him her carry-on bag, explaining her lost luggage situation. She was grateful that she had had her hair cut into a short style that needed not much care, so thus although her "badge picture" would not be what you would call attractive it wouldn't be horrible either, and she did look a bit more sophisticated with the highlighted short hair, which had been Helen's suggestion. The cruise director's appearance however was making her feel old and dowdy. She decided she would treat herself to a spa appointment on the ship as soon as possible. After all she told herself, she was worth it and she was determined to make this trip both productive and enjoyable, perhaps she just may soon need a picture for the jacket cover of her new book if Sergio truly came through for her. She had to smile at her own ambitious dreams.

Half an hour later she was on a tour bus on her way to see her first Hawaiian volcano, actually her first ever volcano. The tour also included free time to explore and walk in the hardened lava fields, a rainforest, and through a 400 year old lava tube. She took lots of notes and was sure she could find pictures to accompany them from the ship's photographer before submitting her first article as he was clicking away at photos which she knew from her previous shore trips with the cruise line would be displayed for purchase that evening after dinner in the Photo Gallery on the ship. She would of course have to clear their use for publication with both the line and the photographer, but imagined that would not be a problem if the article provided positive publicity.

When she arrived back to the ship the security guard as promised presented her with all her boarding documents and returned her passport that she had entrusted to the cruise director to get the paperwork started. The Isabella was a smaller version of the Columbus and so she found her way quickly to the travel desk, feeling a bit more comfortable than when she had first boarded the cruise ship in Barcelona. That seemed like many years ago now. She signed the requisite documents, chose her table seatings, signed for upcoming land tours and received her cabin keys. When inquiring whether her luggage had arrived from the airport the answer was a disappointing negative. The clerk assured her that these things happen and airline had the ship's port schedule and would have Aloha Air deliver the luggage as soon as it arrived. However, thankfully her shipped luggage from Barcelona was on board.

Due to complete exhaustion and a desperate need for a good night's rest, she ordered room service for dinner, took a quick shower and sat on her balcony with a glass of wine watching the lava trickle down the side of the mountain from the volcano 4000 feet above as they pulled out of port on the way to their next stop.

She slept until almost noon the next day as it was a sea day. Her new life was beginning, or should she say the newest chapter in her new life. She was not sure what the future would bring, but she was open and ready to embrace it, and would continue to write to Kara every week detailing events and thoughts so if she ever chose to find her mother she would know that she had never been out of her thoughts. In fact she wrote to Terri and Kara as she sipped on coffee on her balcony and stared at the huge expanse of water in front of her.

My dear friends:
I continue to treasure every picture and letter you send and am always comforted by the bright shiny smile on Kara's face and the obvious joy in her eyes. She is a beautiful child and I am most grateful that since she cannot be with me that she is with the most loving couple I know. Your joy as a family is palpable in your letters.
My newest venture is beginning……

With this she filled them in on her latest travel news, her still shaky emotional state, but her renewed vow to become a well-known author with all profits going to Kara one day. She ended by saying:

You are probably aware that Andrew is in town with Jenny as a write this and you may have already run into him at some point at the club. I will be anxious to know how that visit goes, and if he runs into Kara at all during his short visit. I trust your secrecy, however do wonder if he will see any resemblance when he meets her, with those gorgeous brown eyes which are so obviously his!

Her letter to Kara simply told her once again how much she loved her, how she was never out of her thoughts, and then described for her the dolphins she was seeing off the port side of the ship. Hopefully some day in the future she would read this letter. It was hard to imagine that she was already 2-1/2 years old. She had to be careful as she sealed the envelope not to let her tears smudge the address on the envelope.

Next stop Maui. She had read some about the famous beaches of Maui, the Hawaiian luau as a "must do" for a first timer to Hawaii on any hotel or cruise agenda, etc., and she was determined to make the most of her one day there. She wanted to write about something other than what was already in every other ship's brochure.

With this in mind instead of taking one of the many tours available at the dock. She decided to take a city bus into the main beach and shopping area. Nothing like a little local flavor.........The bus was crowded and stopped at almost every street corner, as this was the route the working man/woman used each morning. She began taking notes watching the streets go by and listening to people's conversations. It took about an hour to get into the "tourist-y" areas and upscale shopping center, along with the upscale hotels and famous Maui beaches. Well of course she had to cover this in her brochure also, and for the "sake of research" proceeded to the shopping center to buy herself an appropriate Hawaii bikini. At least that is what she told herself. She was actually quite proud she could still wear a bikini at age 40 and the mother of a two year old child. Yes, she was returning slowly to her normal self she thought.

She took a quick dip in the ocean and then donning her new beach cover-up, took a seat at the closest hotel beach-bar and ordered an ice-cold beer. She tried to direct her thoughts to the article she would write for the cruise line, but also kept her ears open to the bits of conversations around her, with her 'writer's ear' always listening for new ideas/plots for the next mystery novel. Having finished her drink she took a leisurely stroll down the beach. She was finding quickly that it was hard not to feel good in Hawaii.

When she got back to the ship she found a single orchid in a vase with a small note on the desk in her cabin. The note read "You cannot imagine my pleasure at finding out you were sailing with us these next couple of weeks. I have made reservations for Fleuris, the onboard French restaurant, for 9 p.m. and am hoping you will join me."

It was signed, Mark Blanchard.

Though she strongly suspected Andrew's involvement in Mark just happening to be on this ship, she was overjoyed at the thought of seeing him again. She remembered how he and Sasha had visited her in Barcelona whenever their schedules allowed to help her out of her depression following Kara's birth. She didn't even think twice before returning the call, leaving a message and accepting the invitation. She was both exhausted and hungry, she could never refuse a French meal, and after all part of her job was to write about the meals on the ship wasn't it? She took a wonderfully long hot shower and opened the bottle of Chardonnay that

Andrew had arranged to have delivered to her cabin on her arrival. As she sat on the balcony watching the ship pull out of port she began to relax. Yes, it would be lovely seeing Mark again.

After a quick embrace and the requisite "You look great" comments exchanged between two old friends who had not seen each other in almost a year, they settled in at a secluded table in the corner. Mark wanted all of their attention focused on one another with no interruptions or distractions allowed.

"That was very thoughtful of you to think of me tonight" she said as she sat down, "how did you know that French food is my downfall, I gain weight just smelling the sauces no less the deserts?"

Mark grinned as he pulled out the chair for her. "I also happen to know that mussels, white wine, and a chocolate soufflé are high on the list."

"Oh dear, now I am thinking that you have some inside information." She said this half kiddingly but by now she had stopped even being surprised by the things Andrew could make happen, and of course what information he must also share with people. She had looked at the employee listings in her researching the Isabella and had not recognized anyone. How could she possibly overlooked Mark's name?

"How did I not see your name on the staff roster? I specifically looked for Sasha's or your name but then I thought that would just be too coincidental and wonderful to expect."

"OK, if we are going to renew an honest friendship over the next two weeks I must tell you that

Andrew called the ship and wanted to assure that you got royal treatment for the next two weeks, so I thought I would take on that assignment myself."

She wasn't sure if she was flattered or upset that Andrew felt he had to still help her manage her daily life. Even though she was indebted to him financially, a problem she intended to resolve as time went on, she felt she really needed to be totally on her own for perhaps the first time in her life.

Over a bottle of very good French white wine Mark proceeded to explain that he was on a month's hiatus in Hawaii between cruises when Andrew called and said she would be traveling on the Isabella and resuming her writing. So, I decided to hitch a ride, one of the perks afforded staff when there is room on a ship, and hoped you wouldn't consider me an intrusion. Sam Allen is the official cruise director for this voyage.

"Andrew said you could fill in any details you chose, he just felt you might appreciate an insider's perspective while seeing the islands for the first time. I was more than excited to oblige."

Her first thought was: is it possible that Andrew was "matchmaking" now that his romantic interests had taken a different course, but she quickly dismissed that and felt he was just being protective of her. Did he see himself as her self-appointed big brother? How strange was that twist?

"Andrew is an old friend as you know and that is very sweet of him, but you truly don't have to watch over me. I am perfectly capable of taking care of myself, albeit I am feeling somewhat of a novice at this after my long hiatus on land."

"Well, I have been cruising the islands for the past year and so if I can help with anything let me know, I certainly don't intend to play chaperone or inhibit your freedom in any way." The irritated, and yes somewhat disappointed tone in his voice was hard to miss.

"Forgive me, that was really rude of me. I would of course enjoy hearing your views on the islands, what is worth seeing and what is not etc., it is also nice to have a dinner companion at the end of the day." She tried her best at flirting innocently, something she hadn't done in quite some time.

"Are you still in touch with Sasha, is she still cruising with you occasionally? Seems I have lost touch with her the last few months." Carolyn tried to keep the chatter light.

Mark explained that Sasha had gone back to the States, and with Andrew's help had found a job at a small hospital in Northern Virginia where she was feeling "more useful."

"Andrew's connections never cease to amaze me!" was all Carolyn could manage to reply. She seemed to be repeating this phrase a lot in the last couple of years.

"So, what were your impressions of Maui today?" Mark lightly turned the conversation to anything but what would seem like too personal or too intrusive. They discussed the shopping on Maui, the beach scene, and of course the all too "fake and touristy" atmosphere of the hotel luaus.

The rest of the evening they turned their attention to the food, and a lovely meal it was. They ended with some brandy out on deck under a perfect star studded sky with seas as smooth as glass. She was beginning to think she could get accustomed to this life adventure.

"This has been a delightful start to my Hawaiian adventure Mark, I would love to get together and pick your brain about the cruise ship, the islands, the schedules etc. etc. whenever you are free." She couldn't believe she was being that forward, but after all the wine and after dinner drinks and of course the fact that he did look kind of like a young Harrison Ford with a very impressive swagger. If Andrew's intent was to put them in each other's path she just might enjoy the experience. What was the harm in having some fun on this adventure while learning a bit, she had already researched Hawaii in the literature, but nothing was as informative as hands-on learning from someone who knew the territory.

She awoke to a slight breeze coming in from the balcony where she had propped open the door with the desk chair so as to smell the ocean and listen to the waves as she slept, a secret she had learned on her earlier cruises after reading the authoritative sign on the glass warning to keep the balcony doors closed tightly, a safety precaution against wind and ocean spray getting into the cabin in case of rough seas. No worry, there was barely a ripple on the water below. She quickly removed the chair, closed the balcony door and donned her robe before answering the knock on the door. When you order coffee and juice to be delivered at 8 a.m. she had learned quickly on her previous sea voyages, the service is prompt.

She sat on the balcony sipping the coffee in a slight fog before realizing that she had not written her weekly letters to Terri or Kara. She ordered another pot of coffee and some danish and corrected that immediately.

The ship had made two more stops since her first night dinner with Mark, and true to his promise he only showed up to help out with local information when invited. She had actually begun to wonder if he was relieved not to feel responsible to Andrew for her having a successful voyage. Now they were on the two day voyage to the tiny island in the south pacific that would be their "requisite" foreign port before being allowed to return to the American Hawaiian Islands.

It was on the second of the two sea days on the long voyage to Fanning Island when the call came through. It was Sasha and she sounded both nervous and excited. She explained that Mark had informed her that she was on the Isabella.

"Sarah, I had to talk to you before you hear of this life-changing decision I am making as I don't want to chance losing your friendship." She went on to explain how she had left the cruise line and with Andrew's help had relocated to Northern Virginia, which Carolyn already knew from her conversation with Mark. During course of the phone call Sasha explained that she had gotten a very unexpected call from Jeff Mullins. It seems that when in Barcelona she and Jeff had talked some about her discontent with the direction of her nursing career. She had loved at first the adventure of the free travel, but the novelty was wearing off. She had explained to him that although she was grateful to have been able to see glimpses of many ports around the world, she felt it was time to change her career path. She did not know in what direction that decision would lead her, but she did know she needed to do more than catering to cruise passengers with their seasickness, headaches, occasional colds and stomach problems, the anxiety of the first time travelers etc. Perhaps in the future that would be a great 'retirement' job, but not at this stage in her life. Bottom line was she had kept in touch with Terri and Jeff over the past two years and in one of Terri's letters she mentioned that she wanted to leave the office and stay at home with Kara and enjoy her growing-up years. When Jeff heard she had left the cruise line and was actually in Northern Virginia, Jeff called to see if Sasha would be interested in coming to work for him so that Terri could be more of a full time mom.

"I am going to start next month. I have given my notice at the hospital and I will rent a car and drive to Charlottesville on Monday to get settled. Terri and Jeff have found an apartment for me to rent close to the office."

Carolyn sat down as she absorbed the news. Her first thought was that her best friends had adopted her daughter, and now her new-found relatively recent friend of the past couple years would also be sharing in Kara's life. She was both excited with the connection that it provided her with Kara's life, and also depressed and saddened once again that she could not be part of that life.

"Please say it's okay with you Sarah, I feel like I am doing something behind your back but at the same time am very excited to restart another life for myself."

"Of course it is okay with me, actually has nothing to do with me." She found herself saying. "I am just surprised that Terri has not mentioned any of this to me in her letters."

There was a slight pause before Sasha said "Actually I asked her not to say anything, I wanted to be the one who told you as I knew your first thoughts would be of Kara and the fact that you could not be part of her world, while your friends would be. It just somehow feels wrong in a way, and I know you must be hurting."

Like the true friend she was, Sasha had read Carolyn's thoughts exactly. Question now was would Terri and Jeff be cable to call her "Sarah" in front of Sasha or would they trip-up and call her Carolyn…this latest move did complicate life just a bit more.

Sasha and she exchanged a few more pleasantries and details about the arrangement before hanging up with promises to keep in touch with each other. As it would turn out, Sasha became another lifeline to Kara and something of an "older-sister-friend" to Kara as the years went on.

Carolyn sat dazed for a while just staring out at sea. This newest development frightened Carolyn a bit if she were honest with herself. It was still only Terri and Jeff who knew of Kara's biological parents. However, now Sasha and Andrew had connections to the area and they both knew at least Sasha's biological mother's history. She jotted a letter off to Terri voicing her concerns. After the initial pleasantries, update on her status, and questions regarding Kara, she got to the real reason for this particular letter:

> *...Today I received a call from Sasha that she is going to work for Jeff. The web grows larger and I fear someone will slip up by revealing hidden information...calling me "Carolyn instead of Sarah" in front of Sasha... or in a million other small ways...*
>
> *I don't mean to sound bitter, as I know my part of this bargain was to stay out of things and allow Kara to grow up in a loving family with a normal childhood, it is just so hard knowing that my closest of friends are now becoming part of Kara's life, while I am not.*
>
> *On the other hand Terri, I am grateful as always, and very happy for you and Kara that you will be free from work duties and will be able to spend more time together during her growing up years.*
>
> *I will look forward to hearing all the latest news. I have enclosed as always my latest letter to Kara.*

"So explain to me again the purpose of this journey to Kiribati." She and Mark had called a truce on their sarcastic interchanges and decided they were truly enjoying renewing their friendship. She had not mentioned Sasha's situation again and instead had reverted to a lighter subject. Carolyn would deal with her own fears and feelings in private. She thought of Scarlett's famous line in Gone With The Wind: "I'll deal with that tomorrow." For now she back to living in the present.

"I just don't understand why we have to leave the islands and spend four days at sea, seems like a loss of precious sightseeing time to me."

He glanced over the top of his glass at her and said, "I will bet you dinner at a restaurant of your choice when we get back to Honolulu that you will be very grateful to have taken this little side trip. It is my very favorite island to visit.

They had formed the habit of meeting in the top deck lounge at sunset on sea days to recap the day's activities. It was not only relaxing but he was able to give her some little known facts and sometimes humorous bits of information about the island she was writing about for her article on any particular day, sometimes even contributing to her "mystery series" with some thoughts or ideas to include in the novel regarding the days at sea, or an interesting port visit.

"As you know, we are sailing on a ship that is registered in Italy. There is a little known regulation in place that basically says any ship not registered in the United States cannot sail from an American port back to an American port without making a stop at a foreign port in-between"

She looked at him with a totally bewildered expression.

"I imagine it is something to do with promoting the American cruise line business," he explained. "However," he continued, "as you will soon see it has become a favorite stop on this particular route for a lot of people."

The next day would not only prove Mark right regarding the island but also start a new chapter in the life of Sarah Church.

FANNING ISLAND

She sat on her balcony, coffee in hand, and watched the tiny island come into view. She was still a bit doubtful about the value of this side trip, but decided to keep an open mind. Mark had informed her that this was the closest foreign port they could travel to before re-docking in Honolulu. To her the nation of Kiribati just looked like an isolated tiny group of islands with their destination of Fanning Island being one of the smaller ones. Oh well, she was here and she was going to get as much out of this side-trip for an article as she could. Mark had proven a reliable informative guide so far so she would trust him on this one, and as a bonus she found herself truly enjoying his company.

She met Mark at the third level exit where the tenders would take the passengers onto the island as the water was much too shallow to get the ship any closer to this collection of islands called The Republic of Kiribati. As a staff member, even though on vacation at the moment, Mark had arranged for them to board one of the first tenders before the onslaught of passengers started boarding in about two hours. These early trips were for the crew to bring all the beach rental toys and food and drinks the passengers would be enjoying throughout the coming day. She was immediately impressed while riding the tender into the island as the water was a spectacular iridescent greenish blue that you could see through straight to the bottom white sand. Colorful fish abounded below the surface. Just the ride in alone was spectacular. It was the most peaceful place she had ever seen, just a quiet tiny island, part of the group of small pacific islands making up the nation of Kiribati. Mark explained that the trade ships on their way to the Hawaiian Islands and on to the ports of the west coast of the U.S. mainland would drop off food and other needed supplies usually bi-weekly. The inhabitants had the use of electricity for four hours each evening.

"Let me show you the beach" Mark took her hand as they disembarked and followed a sandy path around to the other side of the tiny island. The native inhabitants were starting to set up their small crafts to sell to their visitors as they disembarked and walked along the only available path to the beach in the sheltered cove ahead. None of the natives spoke English, but gestured their greetings of welcome as they passed.

"I don't think I have ever seen anything quite so isolated and so beautiful! Carolyn remarked as they approached a small cove covered with pure white sand and surrounded by the clearest turquoise water she had ever seen. They sat quietly under some trees and watched while the crew of the ship along with some hired inhabitants soon transformed the beach into a "tourist" area with umbrellas, beach chairs, and greatest of all some "water toys" including rafts, floats, and even small hobbycats belonging to the cruise line. Of course also the requisite beer, "beach drinks" and food stands.

"Wow, now this is worth writing about. Tell me as much as you know about the history of this place!"

A few hours later she found herself on a small hobbycat actually sailing for the first time in her life. The native inhabitant whom they had hired to teach them the intricacies of sailing spoke no English and so sat grinning at them as they maneuvered the sails to catch the small winds and keep the craft moving. He was very lean, had few teeth, finger-nails and toe-nails so long they extended out at least an inch curved around from there, and yet he looked like the happiest and most contented human being she had seen in quite a while. They communicated easily just with sign language. Mark mentioned that the few American dollars they gave him for being their guide for the afternoon would be his income until the next ship came in. She knew she had to find out more about this fascinating place.

BACK AT SEA

"I was so happily in another world yesterday I forgot to tell you about Sasha's call." They were on their two day journey back to the Hawaiian island chain and she and Mark were in the lounge for their "sunset" before-dinner meeting. They had each retired to their cabins immediately upon returning to the ship the previous day, exhausted from both the physicality and the emotions of the previous day. Somehow after their little sailing adventure and a few beers on the beach, they had found a small private cove and fallen into each other's arms. Carolyn had sworn she would never start another relationship, yet here she was fascinated by this man and once again embracing the mantra of 'living in the moment and seeing where life leads me' she thought to herself. How strange that her first sexual encounter since having Andrew's child was actually with one of his closest friends! She could not let those thoughts enter her mind right now.

"If you are going to tell me about her moving to Charlottesville, I already know. It's just that she wanted to tell you herself." Mark could tell this was not going to be an easy conversation.

"Why is everyone still always protecting me and even censoring how I get my information? Do I really seem that emotionally fragile?" Carolyn ranted on and on about how she had turned a corner in her life and was just fine, and she was ready to deal with truth and realities. But was she? After all here she was ranting and raving about how emotionally stable she was to a man with whom she was beginning a relationship and he did not even know her real name or truly much about her at all. However he did know about the most important part of her life, the birth of Kara.

"Sasha has had a hard year and I think she just didn't want to lose the connection she feels to you. She was afraid of what you might think of her being so close to your daughter and watching her grow up when you cannot be there."

Mark continued on, "Remember when you asked me at the beginning of this voyage if I had been in touch with Sasha and if she was still cruising with me. I told you she had decided she wanted to take a break from cruising and Andrew had found her a job in a Northern Virginia hospital? Well, I am afraid that was only a part of the truth."

Mark's expression was strained as he continued, "Sasha's adoptive parents died in a car crash right after you saw her last year in Barcelona. She didn't want to tell you because you were in such a fragile state and had enough problems, but she did talk with Terri and Jeff quite a bit over the past year. I think they became sort of surrogate older siblings to her and the friendship developed after that over the past year. Sasha spent some time with them after settling her parents' estate, and when Terri made the decision to stay home with Kara, it seemed the perfect opportunity for a change of scenery and a new start."

"Why didn't she contact me, she should have known I would be there for her emotionally at least if I could not be there physically? She did not even tell me about her parents' death when we spoke last week! You all need to stop protecting me, treat me as the adult I am and stop, and be truthful with me!!" Even as she blurted this out in her hysteria she realized how foolish this statement was as she was continuing with lots of secrets of her own.

The tears flowed as Carolyn said, "I have been selfishly wallowing in my own problems these past couple of years and not even thinking of others. Mark, I want you to promise me no more 'sheltering Sarah' from the outside world. I am fine, and strong enough to take on whatever comes to be, and I also want to be there for my friends, especially for those who were there for me."

Carolyn looked directly into his eyes as she said "So, no more secrets, okay?" and cringed as he said "Deal, no more secrets Sarah."

And so Mark Blanchard and 'Sarah Church' began a relationship that was to last for many, many years, with no mention of 'Carolyn Blackstone'.

CHARLOTTESVILLE
VIRGINIA
1982

Andrew and Jenny had just finished a round of golf with the owner/developer of a new start-up country club and housing development in Charlottesville. Jenny was being true to her word in introducing new possible clients, and Andrew was promising to help him in the marketing of the real estate end of it in major east coast cities such as NYC, D.C., Baltimore, Philly and other northeastern areas. The golf had gone well and he feeling refreshed after the exercise and happy with his latest Charlottesville connection. He entertained a fleeting thought about how hard it must have been for Carolyn to leave this idyllic little town. It was a beautiful afternoon and he and Jenny were lunching together on the outdoor patio of the 19th hole. He knew he was taking the chance of running into Terri and Jeff, along with Kara, and though in front of Jenny he would have to pretend never to have met them, he was unprepared when he saw them sitting across the patio with not only Kara, a seemingly bright and happy toddler, but also with Sasha whom he would also have to deny a connection. He wondered also how much she knew of Carolyn's history in Charlottesville. Just as he was trying to decide whether to go over and say hello he saw another gentleman approaching their table and realized with a start that it was Roger.

"Hello Andrew, Roger Blackstone," Roger said in a bit of a cool tone as he extended his hand to Andrew and then bent down and kissed Jenny on the cheek. "Jenny didn't tell me you were visiting. I assume you remember me from our golf outing couple of years ago."

"Of course I remember, it was my first visit to Charlottesville and it was very kind of you and Carolyn to make me feel completely welcomed." He wanted to get off the subject of Carolyn as quickly as possible, but felt he had to acknowledge the situation, so continued, "Jenny has filled me in on the divorce, I was sorry to hear that as you seemed perfect together."

Roger smirked and said, "I don't suppose you have kept in touch with Carolyn over the past few years since you had recently just gotten reacquainted as I recall the last time I saw you?"

"Unfortunately not," Andrew lied.

"We certainly intended not to lose touch but our lives once again went in separate directions after the visit here. It had been great seeing her, however my life is spent half-time in London and D.C. and the rest of the time seeing as much of the world as I can. As you know, Carolyn was more the 'settling down' type and seemed very happy in her small town life." Now he really had to get off the subject as he had obviously inadvertently insulted the small town life that Roger too preferred to live, and that he thought his wife had apparently not as she disappeared from his life so suddenly.

While Roger and Jenny made some social plans for the week, Andrew saw over his shoulder that Terri, Jeff, Sasha and Kara were leaving. Probably just as well, Andrew thought, before he encountered another possibly awkward conversation.

Terri actually had seen Andrew and wanted to leave quickly before he spotted them as she didn't want to take the chance that he would possibly see a resemblance in Kara to himself, and thus endanger their custody arrangement. She knew that was selfish, but she loved this child too much to give her up to anyone, not even her biological father.

TEN YEARS LATER
1992

Over the next 10 years Carolyn traveled to many ports with the Italian cruise line, writing for their advertising publications, as well as pursuing a line of mystery novels centered around "Kara," the young cruise ship nurse and her adventures on the high seas, that Sarah Church was now known for. She had constantly researched the ports they were to visit and updated the information for the travel brochures. On the "repositioning" voyages across the Atlantic and Pacific and in her down time between sailings she had used the time to write her mystery novels. The travel writing for the cruise line was a good secure job and she had done well for herself, but it was her mystery novel series that had really paid off. She was quickly becoming independently wealthy and over the past 10 years had paid Andrew back all the money he had lent to her in the early years. She could never repay the consistent emotional support he provided, especially in establishing her new identity. She and Mark had never married but did buy a small condo in Maui together where they would meet whenever their schedules allowed and where they would spend many happy hours together. He also kept a house at Hawk Cay in the Florida Keys.

She had gotten in touch with Sasha shortly after the Hawaiian cruise and they renewed their friendship through letters and phone calls. For obvious reasons Carolyn couldn't visit Charlottesville, but at least she could provide long-distance moral support. Terri continued to keep her appraised of Kara's growing-up years, although the letters did arrive further and further apart. Carolyn continued to write to both she and Kara weekly. Hard as it was to believe Kara was now 12 years old and soon entering her teen years. Carolyn was having a hard time having missed so much of her daughter's growing up years. In never became easier for her.

She finally gave up regular cruising although occasionally when a new ship arrived on the scene, or an old one with sentimental ports she once again gave into her longing for the sea that had been created on those early voyages and booked a room, not as an employee but simply as a passenger enjoying a hiatus from "real life" and gathering more ideas for her mystery series. She also did some "repositioning cruises" where the ship would travel in the off season across the ocean from Miami to Barcelona in order to restart a Mediterranean cruise. She used those 4 or 5 days at sea to work on her novels with no interruptions. She would secure an upper deck cabin and just enjoy the peace and solitude of her total isolation. Since these were "one-way" cruises she would often contact Andrew and visit him in London before flying back to Miami to meet Mark at his place in the Keyes, and on to her home in Maui. Andrew and Helen had gone their separate ways and Andrew was working and traveling as much as always. He continued to live his life happily uncommitted to anyone.

She and Mark also used Hawk Cay as their rendezvous spot whenever he was free and she was on the east coast. It was a tiny key, with a lovely marina, beach, fresh seafood, and bike trails. They often rented a small sailboat and reminisced about their time on Fanning Island many years ago when they both enjoyed their first experience with sailing. She could hardly believe that at 50 she was once again having a satisfying, close, sexual relationship! No permanent commitments, just sharing time together when they could….who would have thought she could be this content, she smiled to herself as she watched the sunrise off her own private little beach. Well, almost completely content except when she would encounter a child of Kara's age at the pool with her mom, or shopping, or conversing on the beach….all the things she never got to do with her own daughter.

As for Andrew he continued to help her with connections in the publishing industry, gave advice on her first draft of each new novel in her mystery series, and even the occasional holiday together, but just as good friends. She could not afford to spend too much time with him as the closer she felt to him the more she wanted to let him in on Kara and the life his child was living. She vowed she would never and could never do that. She had made her decision many years ago and would stick to it until the end. She also knew that she could never let him stray entirely out of her life ever again. She looked forward to their occasional times together, but not in the same romantic way she did with her time with Mark. She would be forever grateful to Terri and Jeff as Kara could not have had better parents.

SASHA'S VISIT

"So obviously Sasha knows of our relationship?" Mark's voice brought her back to the present, they were sitting on his tiny beachfront watching the sunrise, coffee in hand. Life was good.

"Yes, as you know we have been in touch by phone and letters over the last few years, but it will be nice to see her in person. I thought you might enjoy seeing her also."

"Of course, but I think I will bow out after a day or so and let you have some 'girl-time' together if you don't mind." He said as he stretched out in the beach chair.

True to his word, after the three of them had visited for a couple of days, Mark announced one morning at breakfast that he was going to drive up to Miami for a couple of days.

"So, we have a couple days left together, anything special you would like to do or see?" Sasha and Carolyn were sharing a bottle of Pinot Grigio with some fresh fish and salad on the patio as the sun started to settle to the west.

"The sightseeing, the reunion with you and Mark, has been great," Sasha smiled, "How about just some long lazy days, perhaps bike rides, and girl-talk this last weekend."

"So tell me again what Kara is like as she begins her teen years."

Sasha sighed, "I have told you all the details I can think of. She is in middle school but is already acting like a full blown high school kid, attending the high school football games on Friday nights, playing field hockey in the fall along with horseback riding, lacrosse in the spring, and tennis and swimming at the club in the summer. She is a happy, intelligent and beautiful young lady."

Carolyn poured some more wine as she said, "I'm sorry the conversation keeps constantly coming back to Kara, I just can't help being excited hearing all the news in person. Terri has been great about pictures and letters but to be able to have a back-and-forth conversation with someone who really knows her has been amazing. Thank you for your patience putting up with all my questions. It feels so reassuring knowing Kara has such good people surrounding her in her life."

"So, what about your life outside the office and the Mullin family, any romantic interests?"

Sasha actually blushed as she answered, "I have met someone at the club who has become somewhat of a permanent fixture in my life."

She went on over the next couple of hours, another bottle of wine and a sunset beach walk, to explain that she had been going to the country club with Terri and Kara over the years and suddenly one year as a "Christmas bonus" they sponsored her for a single membership and paid the initiation fee. It was beyond any life she had ever imagined herself in, but she quickly became involved in a tennis league and continued to spend time with Kara at the pool.

"Now that Kara is almost in her teen phase, suddenly I am looking quite old to her and so I have developed my own friendships though I really don't have much in common with most of the people there."

Bottom line, she had developed a relationship with the tennis pro. "Seems he needed someone a little more reality based than the women clientele he was used to dealing with. His name is Joshua."

There were so many questions Carolyn wanted to ask but knew she couldn't, because after all 'Sarah Church' had never been to Charlottesville. She found herself wanting to know what had become of Roger and Jenny. Her communication with Terri was now strictly about Kara.

They spent the next day riding bikes, stopping at beach-bar shacks for a cold beer and sandwich, then bringing home fresh seafood and salads for dinner. Sasha even shared some ideas for new "plots" for her upcoming novels based on some of her real life medical emergencies while working for the cruise lines. Carolyn began to feel the renewed closeness to Sasha that she had felt when first they met on the Columbus on that Mediterranean cruise that seemed oh so long ago. She only wished she could be entirely truthful with her about everything. Would she ever be able to be honest with the people closest to her?

On their last evening together it was Sasha who forced out the truth. They had finished dinner and had brought a bottle of champagne out to the beach, started a fire in the small cast-iron fire pit, and settled in to watch the stars.

"There is something I have not told you about Kara," Sasha began. "I wasn't sure whether to bring it up or not as it doesn't really mean anything, yet I feel you should know."

Carolyn's heart was racing. Was Kara ill? Was she in some sort of trouble? She simply stared silently at Sasha waiting for her to continue.

"One day while Kara and I were having lunch by the pool she asked me about my family. She had seen the pictures of my adoptive family in my apartment and knew they had been killed in an automobile accident shortly before I came to work for Jeff in Charlottesville, but we had never talked about it."

Sasha took a deep breath as she continued, "It was like déjà vu, she asked me if I had ever had any desire to seek out my biological parents, just like you asked me when we first met!"

Now it was Carolyn who breathed deeply to slow down her own heart that was racing out of control. "What did you say?"

"I didn't know what to say. If I told her the truth, that I really never had any desire to find them, that my adoptive parents were to me my real family, I felt I might be influencing her to never seek you out and thus I would be hurting you. On the other hand, since that was the truth would I not be hurting Terri and Jeff by not saying that?"

Sasha continued on that she simply remarked that no, she had not ever sought them out, she knew only that her biological parents were from a small village in Russia and that they had not felt they could raise her properly and she certainly held no ill feelings towards them as she knew that they felt they were doing what would be best for her, she added that she had loved her adoptive family greatly and felt she had a "normal" family upbringing with them. "Then we got distracted by some of Kara's friends stopping by on the way to the pool and the conversation quickly changed. Kara has not brought up the subject again."

"I just somehow felt you should know that she must be thinking about her adoptive status. I didn't mention it to Terri or Jeff as I didn't want to upset them either, and am hoping if it continues to be on Kara's mind that she will come talk to me again or even better talk to Terri. I toy with the idea of bringing it up with her in case she needs someone to talk to, or perhaps talking to Jeff as I think he would know better how to talk with Kara and be less emotional about it than Terri would. I feel on the one hand Kara may need to talk with someone about the issue, but on the other perhaps it is just teen hormones rearing up emotions of all sorts and that I should just let it pass until she wants to talk about it again."

Carolyn sighed. She needed to think of her daughter first and not herself once again.

"Sasha, mention the incident to Jeff, I trust he will know how to handle it without making it seem a big issue."

She could see the relief in Sasha's face at having someone to share these thoughts with. Carolyn could also see that something else was troubling her.

Sasha took one more sip of champagne before she looked back at Carolyn.

"I need to say one more thing to clear the air between us," she said as she looked at Carolyn. "Kara has started playing golf with the junior girls team at the club. We were looking through the old golf club albums in the women's lounge one day at all the awards luncheons, ceremonies etc.."

Now Carolyn's heart just about stopped. Of course the pictures would mean nothing to Kara, just a bunch of Terri's friends celebrating their sport. But to Sasha, the pictures of her, Jenny and Terri would definitely have been a shock. She could not help but know.

"Obviously Terri and Jeff know your true name and history, and obviously Andrew does as he knew you in college, but does Mark know? Am I the only one who still mistakenly thinks your real name is Sarah Church? Is it possible that Kara already has seen her biological father around at the club but that neither she nor he knows of the relationship?" Sasha rambled on and on about how strange it seemed that Kara was growing up in Charlottesville where her biological mother and possibly father was from, amongst her adoptive mother's former friends, and yet she did not know the connection.

Sasha continued, "I don't want to bring this up with Terri or Jeff, but I would like a straight answer from you, as I have felt we were close since we first met and feel that no matter how hard it is, that friends should be totally honest with each other."

Now it was Carolyn that was pale and shaky as she replied.

"Those many years ago when we first met on the Columbus as you know I was separated from my husband, pregnant with another man's baby, and feeling totally alone in the world and needing to 'disappear' from my former life and start over. Andrew had helped me establish a new identity and I needed to stick with that. I left my life in Virginia behind and *literally became Sarah Church*. It was the only way at the time to keep my sanity and move forward. I could not have any connection to my former life."

She went on to explain that when she made the decision to give Kara up for adoption so she could have the stable life the child deserved, she was willing to risk that connection someday coming to light because she could think of no better couple to raise Kara than Terri and Jeff. She went on to explain everything that had happened minus Andrew's connection to Kara.

"I did what I felt was best for Kara, and felt that the chances of my new identity not being connected to my past life depended on my completely *being* Sarah Church from that moment forward and never looking back."

The tears welled up in her eyes as she continued softly, "I never saw the possibility of anyone from Sarah Church's life establishing a connection to Carolyn Blackstone's former life, except of course Terri and Jeff whom I trusted completely to keep my past secret."

She looked at Sasha as she continued, "No one but Andrew knows of my true name or the location of my past life, including Mark."

"And what about Kara's father? Is he still in the Charlottesville area? Still possibly at the club?"

Carolyn felt the lie swell up in her throat, as she realized she could still only tell her a partial truth. "No, he never had a real connection to the Charlottesville area and traveled quite a bit for his job. I really can't imagine him settling anywhere to be truthful." That was as close to the truth that she could manage.

They talked on into the wee morning hours, now drinking coffee by their beach fire. Carolyn eventually ventured to ask her about Roger, only to find that Sasha knew who he was from seeing him at certain club functions where he would come over to say hello to Jeff, that no he had not re-married, and she knew nothing about his relationship with Jenny except that she did see them together sometimes, again at club social functions that she attended with Joshua. She also had seen Jenny around at club functions where she would come over to speak superficially to Terri, but again she was not really a part of Terri's circle of friends.

"It was truly a chapter of my life that I have compartmentalized and put away, and seems just a part of the distant past. I feel that I am truly Sarah Church now. Perhaps someday I will be able to discuss the truth with Mark, but I am afraid I see no purpose in doing that now. I feel it would only hurt him to know our relationship has been built on half-truths, and would ruin something very good that we have together."

Sasha understood her reasons, but hoped that she would share the truth with Mark someday so that their relationship could continue on a more honest foundation. For the present she assured Carolyn that she would not be the one to disclose anything, that was Carolyn's decision to make.

BARCELONA
2000

Where had the years gone, she was about to embark on yet another voyage, this time again back in the Mediterranean. Sea travel was quite the rage now having become affordable for even the more average traveler than it had been when she had first sailed. This voyage would be on one of the newest in the Italian Line and what was even more exciting was Terri and Jeff were joining this cruise to celebrate their anniversary, and though she had kept in touch with them weekly she had not seen them since Kara's birth. She called the reservation desk and left word to please notify her as soon as Dr. and Mrs. Mullins checked in. She sat on her balcony, closed her eyes and thought back over the events of the past twenty years as she awaited their arrival. This time she was strictly a guest and it was she who was treating her dear friends to a well-deserved anniversary trip. Mark had wanted to join her but she selfishly wanted time totally alone with Terri and Jeff. He understood.

She awoke with a start as the phone was ringing in her cabin and she realized she had fallen asleep while daydreaming about seeing her old friends. She was very excited. She looked forward to providing them the relaxing trip they so deserved. She had done this

Mediterranean route several times now and so would be able to show them the non-tourist-y parts as well as the more famous sites in each port. She would not be writing on this cruise at all, not travel articles nor mystery series, just relaxing with two very good friends, who just happened to be the adoptive parents of her biological child. What strange turns life takes.

"Dr. and Mrs. Mullens have arrived on board Ms. Church, you had asked to be notified." It was the voice from the concierge desk.

"Give me ten minutes and then show them up to my suite please." She had reserved the penthouse suite consisting of two master bedrooms/baths along with balconies, and a living room in-between. This cruise was going to be her treat. It was lovely to be in a financial position that she was able to treat her friends for a change.

She hurried to fix her make-up and hair, called room service to deliver champagne, fresh fruit and some cheese and crackers. This was going to be pure relaxing pleasure for the next 14 days.

"You look absolutely wonderful" Jeff said as he placed a soft kiss on each cheek when Carolyn answered the door.

"How could she look anything but gorgeous spending her life between the south pacific islands and the Mediterranean countries!" Terri smiled and hugged her warmly. "It is so good to finally see you again face to face after all these years!"

Carolyn made herself not start off by asking for all the details regarding Kara's life that she so wanted to hear about in person, instead she vowed to let that come naturally in the course of the ensuing two week voyage. Right now she owed it to her dear friends to make this a truly relaxing adventure for them, their first vacation away from Kara in 20 years!

"Jeff, if you will do the honors of opening the champagne I will then take you on a tour of your 'home away from home' for the next couple of weeks." She said smiling broadly. "How was the trip over?"

Terri's face was flushed with pleasure even before taking her first sip of champagne as she smiled broadly. "Jeff surprised me and we flew over first class! It was incredible. First a warmed cookie, then a bit later steak and roasted potatoes with snap peas, for desert ice cream with any type of topping from their desert cart. Of course all the champagne, wine or whatever to drink; after a short movie, we reclined our seats into a bed with a real pillow and blanket…….and awoke to the sound of the stewardess handing us a complimentary toiletry bag and telling us we may want to freshen up as we would be landing in about 45 minutes! I have never had a flight go by so quickly, I actually can't wait for the flight back."

Jeff laughed. "Well that's a nice thing to say to our hostess whom we haven't seen face to face in almost 20 years that you can't wait to be heading home!"

Terri's face flushed "Oh Carolyn knows I am very excited to be here and can't wait catch up on her life, have a chance to say in person all the things you can't really say in letters, and to see all the sights."

"Well, first thing is you have to learn to call me Sarah in front of people, or they will be totally confused."

"Oh yeah, want to take bets I am the first to inadvertently mess that rule up?" Jeff said as he handed out the champagne."

After exchanging superficial information about each other's lives and of course assurances that Kara was healthy and well, Carolyn showed them around the suite, told them to take a nice shower, nap or whatever and relax. "We will be sailing at 6 p.m. and then have dinner in the Spanish Tapas restaurant. You are after all technically in Barcelona though by the time dinner is served we will be a bit off the coast."

She could hardly contain her questions about Kara's life, she and Terri of course had been exchanging weekly letters but Carolyn wanted to hear all the tiny details of day to day happenings and what Kara was really like, her thoughts, dreams, attitudes etc. etc.. She once again promised herself to let this be a vacation for her friends and not make it too sentimental. She had lots of time for those conversations in the coming weeks.

"Your luggage should hopefully be outside the door by the time you relax and freshen up. I am going to take my laptop down to the library, I will come back and get you for a quick tour of the ship around 5 p.m. as you mustn't miss being on deck when we sail, dress casually as no one gets fancy the first night out, not even the good restaurants."

"She is wonderful, a full grown woman now as you can see."

They were nearing the end of the voyage, almost the identical route of Carolyn's very first Mediterranean cruise so many years before. They had toured Rome, seen the Ephesus ruins in Turkey, the acropolis and other famous sites in Athens, spent a wonderful two days in Cairo seeing the Egyptian Museum and of course the Pyramids at Giza, and now were in the tiny island of Malta, the last stop on what had been a wonderful two weeks. They had spent the day touring Malta, a tiny island who had gained its independence in 1964 after previously been ruled by several nations including Britain, France, Italy and Turkey. They had now found an outdoor café, ordered a wonderful bottle of local red maltese wine with a platter of bruschetta. Terri was showing Carolyn the most recent pictures of Kara. They had talked at length the first couple of days regarding Kara, but then sort of silently agreed to enjoy their present vacation experience to the fullest and live just in the moment. Carolyn had so many questions and wanted to hear all the details of her daughter's life that she had missed, but she also felt she owed it to Jeff and Terri to allow them their vacation time from any worries or concerns they may have about Kara.

"As you know, she graduated from high school and decided to take a year off before college to 'find herself' as several of her friends were doing."

"She is now in Olde Town, Alexandria, working at a small law firm there." Jeff chimed in, obviously not overly thrilled at the plan. "Her year off has now extended into two years."

"Actually I think it is wonderful" Terri continued. "We have made it perfectly clear that the money for her college education is there for her any time she chooses. She is a very level-headed intelligent young lady and I am sure she will make good choices."

"Right," said Jeff with a bit of a downward grin, "None of which she is sharing with us at the moment."

"Jeff's right in that way," Terri smiled. "Though we feel we have a close relationship, I think she shares her more 'inner thoughts', i.e. 'boy/girl' stuff with Sasha whom she regards as an older sister/ aunt. You know, things you have to sort out yourself or with the help of close friends before bringing them up with your parents." The words "your parents" slid off Terri's tongue easily as this is the way Kara thought of them and they of her. Terri had no idea how painful this was for Carolyn to hear.

"We are both thrilled that she has Sasha close by to confide in." Jeff added. "What a blessing it was to have her enter all of our lives."

Carolyn's heart skipped a few beats as she silently hoped one of those "inner thoughts" Kara was harboring now was possibly centered on finding her biological mother. Aloud she merely said, "You have no idea how grateful I am to both of you for making Kara's life safe and happy, providing her with a good solid foundation, and giving her the opportunity to make her own choices going forward."

"I know you and Sasha keep in touch and that she sends pictures of Charles, is he not the most adorable child?" She went on to say how well it was working out for them that Joshua was now the tennis pro at Mt. Vernon in Alexandria, Sasha was teaching aerobics at a local gym, and Charles was 6 years old already. Now Kara was helping care for him just as Sasha had cared for her. Of course Carolyn knew this all from Sasha's letters and was grateful that she was feeding her weekly information on Kara as well.

Carolyn thought again about how much she had sacrificed in giving up Kara, as the one thing in life she had always wanted had been a family.

"Speaking of 'going forward', what is happening with Mark lately?" Jeff gave Terri the husbandly look that quietly said "don't push it…."

"It's okay Jeff," Carolyn laughed as she caught the warning look, "Mark and I are fine. We had a rough spot a few years ago, but resolved our issues and continue on as good solid friends. We share romantic liaisons occasionally if that is what you are asking, but neither of us are making any commitments at this stage of our lives and we are both content with that."

"Now you sound more like your friend Andrew than you do the woman we used to know." Jeff said with a smile. "By the way, where is he these days?"

Carolyn kept her voice steady as she replied "Still working mainly out of London, traveling constantly for both business and pleasure, and absolutely no thoughts of retirement on the horizon. In fact Mark will be meeting me in Barcelona when the ship docks in a couple of days and Andrew is flying into Paris where the three of us will spend some time together just 'catching up' as we old friends periodically do."

"Oh my, would I like to be a fly-on-the-wall listening in on those conversations" Terri joked.

The next day at sea went quickly as they were all packing for disembarkation in Barcelona the following morning.

After a quick breakfast in their suite the next morning and with lots of hugs, kisses and tears, Terri and Jeff left for their 'departure station' on Deck IV where one of the ship's vans would take them to the airport. "This was wonderful, let's be sure that we never again wait so long for an in-person visit," Carolyn said with tears starting to flow down her cheeks as she realized she was looking into the eyes of the only two people on earth who knew her whole true life story. To everyone else some part of her life was a lie. Sasha, Mark and Andrew still did not know who Kara's father was. Mark did not even know her true name.

"We will keep you posted on Kara's life adventures...meanwhile you must keep us posted on your adventures with Andrew and Mark!...seems maybe one or both of them deserve to know the truth, perhaps both at some point?" Jeff smiled as he said it but she knew he was very serious.

She took a quick shower and began to get herself ready. Mark was going to pick her up at noon after the traffic had cleared around the ship and all the other passengers had departed for their proper destinations. They had decided to spend the night in her place before meeting Andrew the next day in Paris. She could not remember the last time the three of them had been together, it should be interesting…

DISEMBARKING
IN BARCELONA
2000

Mark met her on the pool deck as agreed after all the passengers had departed and looked thrilled to see her.

"I really, really missed you more than ever this time" he said as he embraced her. She realized she felt that way also. Was this getting too serious? Was Jeff right, was it time to clear the air and let Mark know the complete truth before their relationship could advance to the next level. Was she ready at 58 years of age to commit to a permanent relationship with the man she now was beginning to feel she truly did want to live the rest of her life with? Would he still want to be with her when he learned the truth about Andrew and Kara?

They sipped coffee as they caught up on the events of the past couple of weeks. Mark had a strange look on his face as she showed him the latest pictures of Kara which Terri had given her.

"What?" Carolyn said as he stared at the pictures.

"Nothing," Mark replied, "I just can't believe she is a grown woman already, and a gorgeous one at that."

After saying her goodbyes and thanks to the proper people on the ship, and promising to send copies of her travel articles to them, Mark and Carolyn departed and headed to her apartment.

"Want to do anything special with our 'day alone' before heading to Paris tomorrow?" Mark said with a gleam in his eyes. Yes, with him sex was still pretty amazing as even at their advancing age he could still 'turn her on' as the saying used to go. She thought with a smile thinking just how nice it might be to truly commit to him. But as quickly as the thought settled in her mind, Jeff's admonition about owing "total honesty" to both Mark and Andrew also settled in. What would be the consequence to their relationship if she did that?

As it ended up they spent the day mostly in bed, no serious conversations, just enjoying each other and catching up on the news since they had last seen each other. They went to her favorite Tapas restaurant for a late dinner, and packed for the upcoming flight to Paris the next morning.

PARIS
ANDREW, CAROLYN, MARK
2000

Andrew met them at the airport. Carolyn could not believe that in all the traveling she had done over the past two decades that she had missed this city. Of course most of her traveling had been to cities located on the cruise line agendas, she had seen a lot of southern France but not the northern 'city of lights.' Not surprisingly she, like most people who visited this city, was enchanted by it.

"I thought we would make this a more genuine experience by staying at a small French hotel rather than the more touristy chain hotels like the Marriott, Hilton etc. if that is okay with you both." Andrew had not changed at all and still loved being in charge. This was more than fine with her.

"I took the liberty of booking two double rooms next door to each other as the hotel is old and small and does not have suites or adjoining rooms. I think you will be charmed by the hotel staff and of course by its location." As he drove he rambled on about how it was within walking distance of not only the American Embassy, but also cafés along the river Seine, and the Musee` d'Orsay on the Left Bank, not to mention wonderful narrow roads to explore by foot and I think the best food Paris has to offer."

Mark and Carolyn smiled at each other as Mark stated, "Wow, my dear, I do think we have picked The Best tour guide ever for our brief Parisian jaunt." In a quite fake British accent.

The hotel was everything Andrew had promised, tucked unobtrusively into the neighborhood on a narrow street, all genuine French-speaking staff (which both Andrew and Mark spoke fluently, and Carolyn decided would be next on her "learning to do" list), small but very clean rooms each with their own bath. A quaint and very small old elevator took them to their rooms, where they agreed to freshen up and meet in the lobby in an hour. Carolyn did not want to waste a minute in beginning her Paris adventure.

It was an easy walk to the river Seine where they found an outdoor café near a bridge where after lunch would take them across the Seine and onto the Left Bank to tour the Musee d'Orsay. Over wine chosen by Andrew they caught up on each other's lives, reminisced over past shared experiences, and talked of present ventures. It felt that the three of them had been friends forever, and Carolyn silently chided herself for feeling the meeting of the three of them together may have been uncomfortable. It was then that Andrew asked: "So, now that you two seem to be in a permanent relationship, any chance you will be making the ultimate commitment and making it legal?"

Carolyn tried to brush off the question lightly, as Mark had been asking the same question lately and she wondered if he had been talking to Andrew about it. "We are very happy the way we are, I think. No need to complicate matters further."

"Just thought I could start looking forward to being 'best man' and make sure that I put the date on my calendar is all," he said with his old familiar smile.

With that, before Andrew could protest, Mark went to find the waiter and pay the bill, ending an awkward moment.

"Mark is a great guy, Carolyn, and you seem so right together. I am very happy for you both." He then continued on, "Of course he knows about Kara's birth, but does he know your true 'back-story', Charlottesville history, real name etc.?"

"Why are you feeling the need to bring this up now Andrew?"

He looked at her very sincerely, "Because I truly care about both of you Carolyn, you are two of the best people I have ever known and I want you both to be happy. I also know Mark deserves to know your entire story from you in case somewhere, sometime he finds out your true history, name etc. from someone else. That someone would never be me, but he would be very hurt if that information inadvertently came from Terri or Jeff or Sasha for instance. I also feel that I want to be completely honest with Mark, and feel that I have contributed to the deception regarding your background."

For the second time that week she was being pressed to reveal herself completely to Mark, first by Jeff, and now by Andrew. Only difference was Andrew did not know she was still also hiding an important fact from him, the fact that he was Kara's father.

Mark returned to the table, "Looks like some serious conversation going on over here, is everything alright? Should I be concerned about leaving the two of you alone conspiring about something behind my back?" Both she and Andrew laughed lightly and the afternoon mood went back to normal. Carolyn decided she was not going to ruin her time in Paris with two of her favorite people by brooding over this identity question and would deal with it later.

The talk went back to Andrew's current life situation as they walked across the bridge to the Left Bank.

"Is there a current special woman in your life, Andrew?" Mark inquired.

"Not special in the way you mean, Mark. Business still takes up a good part of my time, which as you know I really enjoy. I am afraid I have become too good at enjoying my solitary, and perhaps selfish way of life, to think of any permanent changes. I used to think perhaps when I got to this stage I might regret not ever having had a family, but I can honestly say I am content with life as it is."

The rest of the day was spent at the Musee d'Orsay and they all quickly became immersed in the Impressionist on the ground floor and Post-impressionist works, and the Art-Nouveau movement featured on the second level. While Andrew and Mark were still browsing, Carolyn took herself out to the shady sculpture garden in the back and enjoyed her solitude. After the museum tour they had time to wander the streets on the left bank and find a small bar where they were content with appetizers and wine for dinner. They took a taxi back to the hotel due to the late hour.

The next two days were a whirlwind of sightseeing, the Eiffel Tower, Notre Dame, lunch and people watching on the Avenue des Champs-Elysees, and of course the leisurely requisite boat ride down the River Seine and visit to Montmartre. The weather was perfect and Carolyn let herself concentrate on all things French, refusing to let any other thoughts enter her mind.

On their last day Andrew and Carolyn took a day trip to Versailles, while Mark having been there before decided he would just "wander" for the day in a more non-touristy area. Carolyn suspected he was nicely giving she and Andrew some private time together, though she was not sure this was a good idea.

On the ride to Versailles the discussion turned once again to the past she could not talk about in front of Mark.

"Are you still seeing Jenny?" She had not been planning to ask, but was so curious if perhaps he had run into Kara in Charlottesville, she was not sure if Terri would have told her if he had.

"Yes, as a matter of fact I had a meeting in D.C. a couple of months ago and so invited her to come up and spend the weekend. Nothing serious, but she is quite fun to be with and I do owe her for putting me in touch with what have been several very useful contacts over the years."

"I understand Sasha is now living in Olde Towne, do you ever see her?" She might as well ask all the questions lingering in the back of her mind while she had this private time without Mark around.

"No, I am not sure I would even recognize her. Don't forget we only briefly met at Kara's birth, and then when I helped her get the job and move to C'ville to work for Jeff Mullins."

How easily their daughter's name flowed off his tongue and how bizarre that he did not know the connection.

"Do you ever get to C'ville anymore?" The million dollar question inferring of course had he seen Kara lately. From Kara's pictures as an 18 year old how could he not see the secret she had been keeping all these years. Her eyes and her coloring were so obviously his.

"No, not recently" was his brief answer. "I assume Terri keeps you up to date on things, have you ever regretted your decision Carolyn? I am sure Kara has had a wonderful upbringing, but I know it must have been a tough 18 years for you."

Okay, she was getting much too close to crying and telling him the whole truth, which she was not about to do.

"It was the hardest decision I have ever made, but I have convinced myself that Kara had the most wonderful upbringing with Terri and Jeff and that they have been wonderful parents to her. I have moved on as best I could."

"Speaking of moving on, we started to talk about Mark's feelings for you the other day. He really loves you, you know that right?"

This was not the direction she wanted the conversation to go either. Mark had been wonderful over the years and a great comfort to her, and she loved being with him. She also had to admit however that there were still some latent feelings for Kara's father that sprung up every few years when they got together. After every visit with Andrew she once again had to evaluate her true feelings. Since she did not respond, Andrew continued on:

"All I am trying to say is that Mark loves you deeply and if you are thinking of committing completely to each other, he probably should know your real name and background story, as I said before he needs to hear it from you."

With that, thankfully the entrance to Versailles was in front of them and their thoughts became centered on Louis XIV, the Sun King, and his magnificent palace. She again managed to compartmentalize her thoughts and get back to the present moment.

HAWK CAY, FLORIDA KEYS
2002

The past two years had flown by, Carolyn had served as resident writer on a couple more short cruises for the Italian line, and again used repositioning cruises to finish the latest in her mystery novels featuring the "young nurse Kara in her many adventures at sea." She of course was saving an autographed first edition copy of each novel to give to her daughter if and when they were ever fated to meet. She had kept in touch with Andrew and Mark and met with each separately at various points, but never could bring herself to meet with Sasha again as Olde Towne would just put her way too close to Kara, and she did not trust herself to keep herself together and not to reveal the truth to her if they were actually meet face to face. She still owed it to Terri and Jeff to allow Kara to explore her biological heritage if and when she was ever ready.

The situation had now become much more complicated however and she was constantly in conflict about her sworn secrecy. It seems Kara had had a brief affair with a young intern named Gareth at the law firm where she worked and had become pregnant. Gareth was finishing up at Georgetown Law School and returning to London, and neither of them wanted marriage, it had been just that, a brief affair. Kara had not flinched at the decision to keep and raise the child, Kathryn, herself. Terri continued to write frequently and keep Carolyn updated, she and Jeff were present at Kathryn's birth just as they had been 20 years ago at Kara's. Sasha's son Charles was 8 years old now and while he was at school Sasha kept Kathryn during the day while Kara continued to work as a paralegal.

It seemed all the people who had been close to her over the years were now part of her daughter's present life, except of course Kara's biological parents! She was truly struggling once again about her decisions and did not know how much longer she could stay silent.

Mark had invited her to fly to the Keys so they could celebrate her 60th birthday together. He had become so much a part of her that she could not imagine her life without him, but each time he called her "Sarah" she flinched. She knew now that she had to tell him the entire truth.

A week after she arrived, sitting by a fire-pit on the beach after a great lobster dinner and on their second bottle of Dom Perignon celebrating not only her birthday, but also the release date of her most recent mystery novel, Carolyn shared her true name and her past connection to Charlottesville. If they were to proceed together it was going to be on a truly "no secrets" basis.

Carolyn was shocked that Mark seemed to take the news in a most matter-of-fact fashion.

"I am really not surprised at the fictitious identity as you were obviously running away from a past you did not want uncovered. I have lived with that and felt you

195

would eventually feel comfortable telling me about it. I didn't really guess the connection to Charlottesville and to Terri and Jeff, as I really trusted that Andrew with all his secret past connections had somehow found them, creating the perfect couple to be Kara's adoptive parents just as he seems to find the solution to everything."

The edge in his voice was unmistakable as he said, "The really important question is when are you going to tell Andrew the truth?"

The color drained out of Carolyn's face as she looked at him, "What do you mean?"

Mark's eyes met hers as he said softly, "I have seen Kara's pictures that you keep in your room and carry on your phone, her coloring, her eyes, her hair, there is absolutely no doubt about who her father is. I believe Andrew would have shared that with me if he knew."

She cried as she explained her situation so many years ago, her reasons for not telling Andrew, her reasons for letting Kara go, her regrets and yet her complete belief that Kara's life had been better with Terri and Jeff than it would have been otherwise. They talked for hours and made love on the beach just before sunrise. Sex could really still be excellent at their age when such deep love was attached to it…

She did insist that Andrew never know the truth. It had been totally her decision and she convinced Mark it would only cause Andrew pain as he could not have changed the situation then and he could not reverse anything that had happened since. She hoped the three of them could remain good friends even with Mark now sharing the truth.

Carolyn talked about her dilemma about still not revealing herself to Kara now that she was a grandmother, Mark listened for hours and just let her talk without offering a solution. His only comment was, "That has to be your decision too, I will help and be beside you no matter what you decide. I do love you completely as you must know by now."

ONE YEAR LATER
2003

She returned from the bathroom after freshening up before landing. She was sleepy but also filled with adrenalin at the prospect of seeing Kara. Of course Terri had kept her informed of Kara's life with pictures, but she was hopefully about to meet her only child who was now a single mother herself. Kara had chosen to pursue her life for now as a single mother in Olde Town, Alexandria. She did not know all the details but knew in her heart that Kara was making the right decision for herself and her child. Carolyn was not sure whether in her own life situation she had made the correct decision or not. She especially wondered whether she had owed it to Andrew, and to Kara and now to Kathryn, to give him a chance for involvement in their lives. But now she was really getting ahead of herself as she still didn't know if she was even going to have this longed-for opportunity to re-meet her own daughter and meet her granddaughter. She re-read the copy of the letter she had sent Kara asking her to meet with an open mind when her flight arrived in Dulles.

"My dearest Kara:

I know that Terri and Jeff have kept you informed from the beginning of your adopted status. They wanted to be perfectly honest with you and let you know from the beginning how much they love you and have considered you their very own daughter. They also let you know from your early years that when you were old enough to understand that if at any point you chose to search out your biological parents they would help you. They felt they owed you that. You chose never to follow that path and I promised myself I would respect your wishes in that area.

What you didn't know until recently was that Terri and I have kept in touch over all these years as I desperately needed to know that you were healthy and happy in your life. I never intended to intrude into that life and complicate it for you as I knew I had given up the privilege to be part of your day to day life, I tried to be content knowing you were well. All that changed with the news of your pregnancy and the birth of my first grandchild. I know it is presumptuous of me to want to be part of your life now, but I can't help myself. My life has entered the "sunset years" as they say and I feel I must try to know my child and grandchild if that is at all possible. I am not asking of course to re-enter your life as your mother or as your child's grandmother......I forfeited those rights when you were born and those positions have been earned by Terri and I know you and she have a wonderful relationship for which I am so grateful to her and to Jeff for giving you such a secure and happy life. I am hoping though that we could meet and over the course of time develop a relationship of our own and that you will let me discuss honestly the course my life has taken and let me into your inner world, and that you will let me truly know you. I know it won't happen immediately after a 20+ year absence but I am asking you as a start to meet me at Dulles on my arrival so we can attempt to make a start. My date of arrival and flight information is enclosed at the bottom of this letter that I have asked Terri to deliver to you. Perhaps I could enter yours and Kathryn's life as just an old friend of your mother's, Auntie Carolyn. I urgently want to know you and my grandchild even if from afar, and hopefully for you and I to learn about each other before this short lifetime ceases to be. I have wasted a good portion of my life without the most important person in my life, my reason for living all these years, you.

Whatever you decide please know that I have at least built a successful financial career as a writer and have established a trust fund for the Kathryn in your name for her future education and needs. This fund will be yours and hers whether we ever meet or not, that will never change. I know that cannot in any way substitute for not sharing with you my undying love for you every day of the past 20 years, but believe me I have felt such love and happiness for you and for the life Terri and Jeff have provided you. You have been in my heart every moment of every day.

I have also asked Terri to deliver along with this letter all the letters I have written to you personally over the years sharing my thoughts of you and the details of my life. It is up to you if you chose to read them.

Terri and Jeff can answer any questions you want answered prior to our meeting. Hopefully I will see you in a few weeks, I have thought of you every day since you were born and giving you up was the hardest decision I ever had to make but I am still convinced it was the right one for you.

Love, Carolyn (aka: Sarah Church)

Terri had let her know that she had delivered the letter as promised, but could give Carolyn no further information only stating that upon reading it Kara had asked to be left alone for a few days, that she needed time to come to terms with all this news. Terri had complied and of course told Kara she would support whatever decisions she made for the future of her relationship with her biological mother, and also that she and Jeff were there to answer any unanswered questions. She had also offered her the box of correspondence that she had kept all these years containing the letters Carolyn and she had exchanged over the years regarding Kara's growing up years, and of course the ones Carolyn had written to Kara for just this moment in time. She knew this was a lot to digest in such a short time, and urged her to just make one decision at a time, the first being did she want to meet her biological mother.

As the plane began its descent into the airport and Carolyn gathered her belongings she looked forward with both the anticipation of seeing Kara and Kathryn, and with the sinking feeling that she/they may not be at the gate as she so fervently hoped...

The voice from the aisle startled her from her reverie as the man sat down beside her.

"Did you really think I would let you take this step on your own? I have let you handle things your way all these years, feeling that I really had no right to interfere and trusted that you knew the best way to give our daughter the correct upbringing and the life she deserved. But if she is to meet her biological mother, I think it is only fair she also meets her biological father."

"Did Mark........?" She started ...

Andrew shook his head and took her hand in his as he continued, "No. Mark loves you and would never betray your trust. In fact I did not realize he even knew until just this moment. However, how could I ever have not have connected the dots earlier? It was not until I began seeing your pictures of her as she was growing up that I could see myself in her eyes, her coloring...at first I kept denying it could be true, but I think deep down I always knew it was, and trusted that you were doing the right thing for Kara by not discussing it with me. It was the easy way out for me, though I was never sure that was what I really wanted." The tears fell as his eyes said can you ever understand or forgive me?

They sat silently hands clasped together as they stared out the window watching the plane landing and wondering if they would soon actually be seeing their daughter and granddaughter.

TO BE CONTINUED IN
THE NEXT BOOK:
SECOND CHANCE

Made in the USA
San Bernardino, CA
01 July 2018